Awareness prickled over her skin. A sharp inhale brought about a scent of pine mixed with a masculine scent that painted a vivid image of a handsome smile and brown eyes crinkled at the corners.

"Hello."

Squaring her shoulders, Madeline turned and laced her fingers together as she faced Prince Nicholai.

"Your Highness."

He looked incredible. Dressed in a navy suit with a silver tie, his hair combed back from his face, he looked every inch the austere royal. His face was smoothed into an expressionless mask that made his sharp features look more like a statue than those of a living person.

Something inside her chest twisted. She missed the carefree smile he'd given her on the rooftops of Paris, the naked emotion in his eyes when they'd met in the alcove. On those occasions, she'd seen the man behind the crown.

Now, though...now he looked distant. Unreachable. Untouchable.

Dear Reader,

Thank you for reading my debut with Harlequin Romance, *The Prince She Kissed in Paris*! I had so much fun writing Nicholai and Madeline's story. I loved kicking off their romance in Paris since I traveled there with my husband a few years ago. On our last night, we sprinted across the Pont d'Iéna (Jena Bridge) and made it to the halfway point just in time to see the Eiffel Tower light up in all its sparkling glory. My husband, like Nicholai, wasn't impressed when I first told him about it, but told me afterward it was more of a highlight than he'd expected!

I also loved incorporating research on Croatia's Dalmatian Coast into the creation of the fictional country of Kelna. The palace was inspired by Diocletian's Palace in Split, Croatia. The historic charm of Kelna's capital city, Lepa Plavi, mirrors that of Dubrovnik, a Croatian city crowned the "Pearl of the Adriatic" and famous among *Game of Thrones* fans as the filming site for King's Landing.

I hope you enjoy this sweet royal romance and join me again later for Princess Eviana Adamović's love story. Happy reading!

Scarlett

THE PRINCE SHE
KISSED IN PARIS

SCARLETT CLARKE

ROMANCE

Harlequin® ROMANCE

ISBN-13: 978-1-335-59676-5

The Prince She Kissed in Paris

Harlequin Enterprises ULC
22 Adelaide St. West, 41st Floor
Toronto, Ontario M5H 4E3, Canada
www.Harlequin.com

Printed in U.S.A.

Recycling programs for this product may not exist in your area.

My husband, John, my mom, Lori Beth, and my dad, Martin. My kids, Jack and Hannah. Teddy, Joe, Katelyn, Laura, Justin and Sara. My brother Nate, my sister-in-law Kelsey, and Papa Jim. My family and friends around the country (my St. Louis and Portland in-laws, Aunt Julie, Madi, Christina, my brother DJ, nieces Kyrstan and Samantha, Ayme, Ashley and Mama Donna). My Thursday critiquers: Dyann, Dennis, Cathy, Dora, Tenaya, Kristy, Nora, Claire, Goldie, Rod, Jan and Ed. My teachers: Dr. Anne Farmer, Mrs. Flory, Ms. Austin, Mrs. Young, Mrs. Schrock and Mrs. Long. Melodie, Stephanie, Kimberly and Dee Dee, and my Lakeland ladies, Marta, Ashley and Rachael. And to Steve, who will never read this book, and his wife, Lisa, who has excellent taste.

CHAPTER ONE

PRINCE NICHOLAI ADAMOVIĆ braced his arm against the balcony doorframe as the wrought iron beams of the Eiffel Tower lit up with hundreds of sparkling white lights. The display no doubt dazzled the hordes of tourists who, despite the late hour, would be thronging the Pont d'Iéna and surrounding streets to snap the perfect picture.

He'd seen it plenty of times, had frequently dismissed it as nothing more than a cheap trick to attract visitors and romantics.

But tonight, he, too, watched the show.

When would he have the freedom to be in his own hotel room alone again? Without security guards or press or his family lurking about?

Or worse, a wife.

The lights performed one last dance before settling into a steady golden glow. A beacon for all of Paris to look to. One of hope, history and love.

He snorted. Love was for books, movies and the occasional lucky sap who stumbled upon their soulmate. For people like him, love was not always an option. Especially when the law of his country required that he have a wedding ring on his finger before accepting the crown.

A cold fist tightened around his heart. It wasn't enough that he would lose his father and take over the ruling of a country growing far faster than anyone had anticipated. No, he also had to tie himself to someone he didn't love. All because of an archaic decree.

He quelled his anger as he turned away from the window and crossed the room of his luxurious penthouse suite to the bar. One of the benefits of this night alone was being able to indulge in a glass of bourbon without raising eyebrows. He wasn't anywhere close to the level of the President of the United States or the King of England. Hell, there were actors and actresses more recognized by the general public than he was.

But that was all about to change with the construction of Kelna's first major port that would welcome ships from across the world. Multibillion dollar companies were courting his country, pouring money into building new roads, bridges and other infrastructure that would benefit Kelna's people for decades. The media had started to take notice, requesting interviews and snapping the occasional picture of Nicholai, his sister, Eviana, and his father.

King Ivan Adamović of Kelna. A benevolent ruler loved by his children, respected by his staff and revered by his people. The kind of king one wished could rule forever.

He stared down into the amber liquid in his glass. What would the tabloids do if they knew the truth? That if the doctors were right, the Prince of Kelna would be king before the year was out?

He took his first sip, savored the slow burn down his throat. He'd accepted his fate to be king from an early age. He just hadn't expected it this soon. He'd bought into the myth all children wanted to believe about their parents: that they would always be there. Ivan hadn't always been around the way other fathers could be. He was a man who firmly believed in duty. But Nicholai had never doubted he had his father's love and, equally important to him, his father's trust.

He would rule. He had to.

Even if the thought of sitting on his father's throne, of wandering the palace halls knowing he would never again hear the booming laugh or smell the musky scent of cigars smuggled past the royal physician, twisted his chest into knots so tight it hurt.

And, he thought grimly as he wandered back to the window, he wouldn't have the outlets he did now to deal with the loss. The limited freedoms he currently enjoyed would vanish. Nights like this, where his security team slept next door instead of standing guard in the halls and concerns about paparazzi were minimal, would disappear.

His fingers tightened around his glass. A picture of him on his private balcony, brows drawn together, lips pressed into a thin line, had made it onto the front of one Italian publication that favored dramatic headlines and excessive punctuation.

"Kelna's Bachelor Prince!" the title had screamed. According to an "inside source," the Prince was currently unattached but "open to finding someone to share his life and the throne with." The resulting furor, and the number of single women suddenly vying for his attention, had become irritating at best.

Eviana had found it amusing. Nicholai had not, especially when he'd discovered how news of the palace's search had reached the media. A trusted palace aide, Franjo, had let a photographer into the palace under the guise of taking photos of one of the royal art collections. Two months later and the slash of betrayal still cut deep. Nicholai was a private person by nature. Letting his guard down was not something he did easily. That he had relaxed around Franjo, even considered the man a friend and had shared with him that he was contemplating marriage, had made him feel like a fool.

Never mind that Franjo had done it for a mere five thousand euros. All to cover a gambling debt. Had he just come to Nicholai, Nicholai would have helped him.

Neither here nor there.

It was done. It had taught him a valuable lesson. The more Kelna grew, the less he could trust outsiders.

Thankfully, the architecture firm he was meeting with tomorrow had been arranged and vouched for by his father, one of the few people he trusted without reservation. It would be his last event before traveling home to Kelna. With money pouring in, work had already begun on essential projects like schools and bridge renovations.

For one of the few projects that benefited the royal family, a new ballroom, Ivan had requested bringing in an outside organization from the States. Nicholai preferred keeping things within the country. But Ivan had made a good case for it, pointing out that a firm with no ties to Kelna could bring a fresh perspective and help incorporate elements that would appeal to the swell of tourists they were anticipating in the next couple of years. That the lead architect of the firm was an old university friend of Ivan's, one he trusted to be discreet, had helped sway both Nicholai and his sister.

That and an ironclad confidentiality contract. No more gossipy speculation about his love life. No more lurid headlines and photographs of him with various women dredged up from the past, with reporters venturing guesses as to who his lucky future bride might be.

If only they knew the truth. He wasn't just open to finding someone. He had to.

Shortly after his father's diagnosis, the prime minister had approached him. Dario Horvat had served for years. He was someone both Ivan and Nicholai could count on, even if his views tended to be even more traditional than the King's. So when Dario had told him about the Marriage Law, an antiquated law that hadn't been enacted in over two hundred years, Nicholai's initial shock had quickly given way to anger. He'd just found out it would be a miracle if his father made it to next summer. Learning he had to marry within a year of ascending the throne or he'd lose the crown was the last thing he'd needed to hear.

But Dario had persisted. The last five kings had all ascended the throne well into their fifties and sixties, decades into their marriages. Nicholai would be the first king under the age of forty since before the Napoleonic Wars had decimated Europe.

"Your family is respected, Your Highness," Dario had told him. "Imagine the turmoil Kelna would experience if they lost two kings in one year amidst so much change."

Phrased like that, there had been no point in arguing. The law itself was kept quiet. The last thing Nicholai or the palace needed was a bevy of women suddenly vying for the spot of future queen and possibly bringing the wrong kind of attention to Kelna. Marriage would calm some of the concerns and elevate him in the eyes of the traditionalists. It would also give the country something else to focus on besides the loss of their beloved king. A new princess, a royal wedding and above all, signs that despite Ivan's passing, the line would continue. The throne would be secure.

He'd always known he would marry. Had hoped there would be affection, perhaps even love involved. He thought he'd have more time to find someone on his own.

But he didn't. Such was the nature of duty.

Even now, Dario and a select group of trusted advisors were compiling a list of prospective candidates for him to review when he returned to Kelna. A strategic process. One that would identify women compatible with both the Prince and country. In the coming months, they'd find a way for him to discreetly meet the candidates and see if one would do the role of queen justice.

He glanced down at his watch. Ten minutes past eleven. The meeting was scheduled for nine o'clock in the morning. Sleep had eluded him since the doctor had given him Ivan's updated prognosis. On the nights he did manage to fall asleep, he usually woke an hour or two later, his mind racing.

But he at least needed to try. He tossed back a generous gulp of bourbon and started to turn away when a movement on the roof caught his eye.

There. Beneath the light of the Paris moon, a woman sat on the roof of the east wing of the hotel, her back to him. Dark blond hair tumbled halfway down her back. Intrigued, he watched as she turned her head to look at the Eiffel Tower and smiled slightly as she raised what looked like a bottle of wine in a toast before taking a long drink.

His amusement vanished as she turned and scooted closer to the edge of the roof.

God, no. She was going to jump.

He grabbed the handle of his balcony door, then cursed as he remembered his security team had insisted on installing new locks that remained bolted during his stay. His head jerked up in time to see the woman move again. His heart shot into his throat. He didn't have time to call for help. He grabbed the key out of the desk drawer and unlocked the door, running out onto the balcony just in time to see the woman brace her hands on the roof's edge.

"Stop!"

His command was lost to the sounds of traffic below and a brisk spring wind that flung his words into the night. With a quick glance at the roof a dozen feet below, he pulled himself onto the balcony railing, uttered a quick prayer and leaped. For a breathless moment, there was nothing but the air rushing past him. He landed with a jarring thud that made his teeth rattle in his skull.

Get up. Get to her.

He rolled to his feet and sprinted across the rooftop.

"Stop! *Ne saute pas!*"

The woman's head snapped up. She turned, her eyes growing wide as she saw Nicholai barreling toward her. She pushed to her feet, the city at her back, and raised the wine bottle up over her head.

"Don't come any closer! I'm armed!"

He stopped, holding up his hands as his gaze darted between her and the roof's edge. She was slender, a good foot shorter than he was. If he could just get close enough to pull her away, he could probably subdue her and summon someone on the ground below for help.

"I'm not going to hurt you—"

"I can see you still moving. I'm not that tipsy."

The snarky tone surprised him.

"I just want to help you."

"Help me?" The woman glared at him, fierceness radiating off her small frame in palpable waves that, had the situation not been so dire, would have made him smile. "Help me how? By shoving me off a roof?"

"Stopping you from jumping off a roof."

"Stop me from…" Her voice trailed off as she stared at him like he'd sprouted horns. And then she did the last thing he expected.

She threw her head back and laughed.

Dealing with a crazy hulk of a man had not been in Madeline Delvine's plans when she'd sneaked out onto the roof of the hotel that night.

A very handsome, very irritated-looking hulk of

a man she acknowledged as her laughter subsided and he continued to glower at her. With her fingers still wrapped around the neck of the wine bottle, she started to step back and put a little more distance between herself and her unexpected visitor.

His eyes widened.

"Stop!"

Before she could blink, he darted forward with a speed she hadn't anticipated, wrapping his strong arms around her waist and yanking her forward. Their legs tangled and he stumbled, falling backward and pulling her down with him. The bottle slipped from her fingers, hit the roof with a clink and rolled away. She landed hard on his chest.

A broad, muscular chest.

"What are you doing?" she snapped. She braced her hands on his shoulders, intending to push herself away. But her traitorous fingers just curled into the white material of his shirt as a scent that reminded her of wild woodlands wrapped around her.

Her breath hitched. She looked up to see the man watching her intensely.

Wow.

In the chaos of the moment, she hadn't got a good look at him. But now, as her eyes roamed over his face, she realized what a travesty it was that someone who was probably drunk was also incredibly attractive. Dark, wavy hair had been swept back from his forehead, a couple stray wisps curling on his neck. She could only guess at the color of his eyes—green, perhaps?—beneath thick brows currently drawn together in a frown. His strong nose reminded her of a Greek statue, the square jaw softened by the tiniest dimple in the middle of his chin.

The man wasn't just attractive. He was devastatingly handsome.

"You can let go of me now."

Her voice came out husky and breathy. The man's frown deepened as he moved his hands from her waist to her arms, anchoring her against him.

"No. I'm going to call 112 and have the emergency services send someone over—"

"Hey!" she snapped.

The man's eyes widened a fraction, as if he wasn't used to being interrupted, before they narrowed again.

"Listen, ma'am, you—"

"I was enjoying a lovely bottle of cabernet sauvignon, when some rampaging man comes leaping across the rooftops like he thinks he's acting out 'The Murders in the Rue Morgue.' If you need to call the emergency services for anyone, call it for yourself."

His grasp on her arms slackened. She used the opportunity to push herself up and back away. She glanced around and spotted the wine bottle glinting in the moonlight. Keeping the man in her line of sight, she inched over and picked it up.

The man sat up slowly, holding up his hands. "There's been a misunderstanding."

"What clued you in?"

His lips twitched. "I saw you sitting on the edge of the roof. When you scooted closer, I thought you were going to jump."

She shot a quick look over her shoulder and grimaced. From this angle, she could see how the riser she'd been sitting on could look like the edge.

"There's another five or six feet of roof on the other side. I was just enjoying the view." She looked around. "Did you climb up the fire escape, too?"

"Not exactly."

Perplexed, her eyes roamed over the roof. Where on earth could he have come from…

Her mouth dropped open as she spied the open door to the balcony of one of the west wing's penthouse suites.

"You didn't…" That had to be more than a ten-foot drop, not to mention the gap between the balcony and the roof of the east wing. "Did you?"

He stood and grimaced. "That's going to hurt tomorrow."

"Of course it's going to hurt," she retorted. "You jumped off a balcony! You were worried about me jumping off a roof, so you jumped off a balcony and nearly got yourself killed!" She rushed forward and circled him.

"What are you doing?"

"Checking for injuries."

"Are you a nurse?"

"No, but I do have four siblings. We've all done our fair share of patching up each other's injuries."

Nothing looked out of place, no obvious scrapes or bleeding. She finished her assessment and stopped in front of him.

"You should see a doctor tomorrow. Just to be safe."

He looked down at her with a strange expression on his face, as if he couldn't quite figure her out.

"I'll do that."

"Good." She huffed out a breath. "Even though I didn't need saving, that was very heroic."

"I'm not a hero."

She arched a brow. "Maybe you're not familiar with Superman? Can leap tall buildings in a single bound? I'd say that makes you a hero."

His soft chuckle rolled over her, a deep sound that made her pulse beat just a little faster.

"Thanks, Miss…?"

"Delvine." She stuck out her hand. "Madeline Delvine."

His hand engulfed hers and she swallowed a gasp as warmth flowed up her arm.

"Well," she said, pulling her hand back and hoping he hadn't noticed her reaction to his touch, "thank you again for the attempted rescue."

"I apologize for scaring you."

"Thank you, and likewise."

He reached down and picked up a couple things off the roof.

"Yours?" he asked.

"Oh, thank you." She held out her hand for the sketchbook, then frowned as he looked at her drawing.

"This is very good."

Her cheeks flushed. "Thanks."

She'd drawn the tower when she'd first come out on the roof, combining her view with how she imagined it looked from the iconic bridge that arched over the Seine. Even though it had been more whimsical than technical, she'd been pleased with it.

Her would-be rescuer pointed to the couple she'd drawn on the bridge, the man holding the woman tight against his side, their faces turned to the tower.

"Who are they?"

Madeline shrugged. "A couple in love. I imagined them watching the tower light up right before he proposes. Or maybe she tells him they're finally expecting a baby. Happy things."

It was one of the things she loved about her work. Imagining not just the buildings themselves, but the people who would occupy the space, whether they were simply passing through or staying for decades.

"You're a fan of 'and they all lived happily ever after?'"

Something dark flowed beneath his words.

"Yes." She grinned. "I even picked up a copy of *Pride and Prejudice* from a bookstore on the Left Bank this afternoon." When his frown deepened, she asked softly, "You don't believe in happily ever after?"

His expression evened out into a mask as smooth as glass and as sharp as obsidian.

"Life isn't a fairy tale."

An answering frown crossed her face. "No." Her ex-fiancé Alex's smug smirk flashed in her mind. Between his misogynistic expectations regarding her role as his future wife and his obsession with his own appearance, he had been more villain than hero.

She pushed thoughts of Alex away. "Doesn't mean there aren't fairy-tale moments."

"Oh?"

She flung out her arms. "You're on a rooftop in Paris under a blanket of… Well," she amended as she glanced up, "you can't see the stars all that well. But still, stars above, the Eiffel Tower in the background, a bottle of wine." She looked over at the iconic structure. Before her mysterious would-be rescuer had charged onto the scene, she had been staring at it for nearly twenty minutes. Traveling to Paris had been at the top of her wish list ever since she could remember. A list she was just now starting to tackle after working her way through her architecture degree and certifications. Never had she thought her career would bring her here, that she would get paid to bring dreams to life in the most incredible places around the world.

If her stepfather could see her now, working in the field he had introduced her to, succeeding like she'd always talked about it, he would be so proud of her. He'd always encouraged her to go after her dreams, to balance her love of family and home with having adventures.

She'd been temporarily derailed by Alex and the box he'd tried to shove her in. But she'd broken free.

Some of her earlier happiness returned. She wrapped her arms around her waist and smiled.

"It doesn't get much more fairy tale than this."

"Don't fairy tales include romance?"

Her eyes darted from the Eiffel Tower back to the man.

"Most do, I guess." *Unless you attract frogs instead of princes.* "But they don't have to." She held up the bottle. "My fairy tale is pretty simple right now."

His lips quirked. *What*, she wondered, *would a full-on smile look like?*

"I don't like leaving you out here alone."

She sighed. "I told you, Mr...." She frowned. "I didn't get your name."

He stared at her, that considering expression on his face again.

"Nick," he finally said.

"Just Nick?"

"Just Nick."

"Well, Just Nick, I'm twenty-seven and can fend for myself up here." She smiled to soften the bluntness of her words.

He walked toward her. Her breath hitched in her chest. In a city swirling with scents, most of them pleasant, some of them not, his cedar-like fragrance crept into her senses once more.

"I don't think a mugger would care how old you are."

"Probably not." She made a show of glancing around. "I don't think too many muggers crawl across the roofs of Paris."

He made a noise that almost sounded like a growl. "I'm not leaving you alone."

"Well then, I guess you'll just have to join me."

As soon as the words were out, she inwardly cringed. What was she doing? Inviting a strange man to spend time with her on the roof of a hotel at midnight? She'd promised herself that she would have an adventure in Paris. But flirting with a man who had just tackled her was a little much. Misguided as his actions had been, he'd been trying to help, not score a date. The last thing he probably wanted was to drink wine with a tourist.

And then he smiled at her. A full-on smile that blew past the walls she'd erected against the male sex after her breakup and sparked a warmth that spread through her body and left her breathless.

"I'd be honored to join you, Madeline Delvine."

CHAPTER TWO

NICHOLAI STRETCHED HIS legs out as he perched on the riser Madeline had been sitting on when he'd first spied her from his balcony. He had to admit, from this vantage point the Eiffel Tower looked larger than life. Even in his brooding, jaded mood, the romanticism of the tower was hard to ignore.

As was the woman sitting next to him. They had been sitting in silence now for several minutes. Unlike most of the people he knew, she seemed comfortable with the silence. She sat now with a small smile on her face, taking an occasional sip of wine and watching the Paris nightlife speed by on the street below. He'd declined her offer of a drink, content to sit and enjoy the moment.

He blinked in surprise. He couldn't remember the last time he had felt content. Certainly not content with something as simple as sitting next to an interesting woman.

And Madeline Delvine was one of the most intriguing women he'd met in a very long time.

He glanced at her out of the corner of his eye.

Blond hair cascaded around a surprisingly strong face. Unlike the few previous women he'd been involved with, who would have accepted compliments like "dainty" and "fairylike" with pleasure, Madeline would most likely laugh that deep, throaty laugh before pointing out her square jaw and straight line of a nose were anything but dainty.

Yet the longer he looked, the more he liked what he saw. Dark brows arched above dark blue eyes. She glanced at him and, when she caught him looking, blinked before ducking her head, a tiny smile flirting about her lips. Full lips were a pleasing contrast to the sharp, elegant slash of cheekbones. Her angled chin made her look feminine and strong and mischievous.

But it wasn't just her unique beauty that caught his attention. It was the simple, deep serenity on her face. All the incredible restaurants, the lauded landmarks, the finest museums just a breath away. And she looked like she'd won the jackpot, sitting on a rooftop drinking wine.

"You have questions."

He blinked as she turned to face him, the little smile spreading into an impish grin that revealed the small, charming gap between her front teeth.

"I do?"

"You keep looking at me like you can't figure me out."

He couldn't. He wasn't recognized on the streets

by many. But having a conversation like this, with a woman who had no idea who he was, who his family was, was a novelty. One that needed to be treated with caution. He would be hard-pressed to believe this had been an act to entice him out onto the roof for paparazzi photos, an interview or even seduction.

But stranger things had happened. He would not walk blindly into a trap. Not again.

"I am trying to figure you out."

"So ask."

"Just like that?"

"Just like that. For example, where are you from, Nick?"

He debated for a moment, then took a leap of faith. "Kelna."

Her wrinkled brow told him he'd been right to assume she wouldn't know about his home country. A challenge to overcome as he brought Kelna to the world stage, but one that, in this moment, he was grateful for. The opportunity, for one night, to be just Nick.

"I've never heard of it."

"It's a little country on the coast tucked between Croatia and Montenegro."

She leaned back, her eyes alight with interest. She offered him the bottle again and, after a moment, he accepted it. The intimacy of placing his lips where hers had just been stirred something in his chest. The wine, dark and velvety, lingered on his tongue as he handed the bottle back.

"Hvala vam."

"You're welcome, I think?" At his nod, her smile grew until her eyes crinkled. "What language do you speak in Kelna?"

"Croatian and English, although there are others, too. Serbian, Bosnian, a little bit of Italian."

"And how does someone from Kelna find himself in Paris?"

His pulse kicked up as his eyes sharpened. Was she digging? But he saw nothing suspicious in her demeanor. No hint of artifice in the midnight depths of her eyes.

"Business."

"Ah." At his questioning look, she shrugged. "I would press for details, but I'm also in Paris on business. My boss swore me to secrecy."

"Oh?"

She laughed. "I'm going to say as little as possible so I don't slip up. J.T. told me very little, except that we have the potential to land a big contract with someone very important. I've never seen him so excited."

"Then we won't talk about business. Is this your first time in Paris?"

"Yes." She sighed happily and tilted her head back. The moonlight kissed her throat, made her skin shimmer with silver light. "It's more than I ever imagined it could be. There are so many places I want to travel. I've only been out of school for a short while, and I'm just now starting to make money," she added with a laugh. "Getting to kick off my traveling adventures in Paris is pretty incredible."

"You're from America?"

"I am. Just outside Kansas City."

"Tell me about it."

Her brief hesitation piqued his curiosity.

"I spent a lot of my childhood along the banks of the river a few miles east." Her smile widened. "My favorite part was watching the fog roll in from the water over the fields in the spring. Although I liked winter, too."

He chuckled. "Was there anything you didn't like?"

Her dimples deepened. "Not really. In the winter the snow dusted everything with white. I'd wrap myself in a thick blanket and sit on a wraparound porch with Paul and my sister Greta."

It all sounded so quintessentially American he couldn't help but smile.

"Who's Paul?"

"My stepfather." She glanced down at her sketch pad. "The first time Paul and I spent time together, just him and me away from my mom, he took me to the Nelson-Atkins Museum of Art in the city." She scrunched up her nose. "I was a bit of a brat to him at first. But instead of making me feel guilty, he asked for five minutes. Five minutes and if I didn't like it, we'd leave and he'd buy me ice cream on the way home."

"I'm guessing it was more than five minutes."

"Two hours. He had to bribe me with ice cream to get me to leave. It was magical." She smiled. "It was where I fell in love with art. And when I started to see what my mom saw in Paul. He was the best dad I could have ever asked for."

"Where is he now?"

"He died. Two years ago." Grief poured off her in a sudden wave. That he could sense it, almost feel her anguish, shocked him. He'd never experienced such a connection to anyone other than his father and sister. Being a royal meant keeping your emotions in check, maintaining control.

He nearly reached out to her and stopped himself just in time. Touching her would just create another connection, one that would further tempt him and make it that much harder to leave at the end of the night.

"I'm sorry, Madeline."

"Thank you. He was nearly twenty years older than my mother. They managed to have three more children. And he never made my sister or me feel like we weren't one of his own."

"Sounds like a good man."

"He was the best. Told me there was nothing I couldn't do. Nowhere I couldn't go." Her smile returned as she turned her head to gaze out over the eastern reaches of Paris. "But as much as I'm loving it here, I can't picture living anywhere but Kansas City. I love adventure, but I also love going back home."

"I know the feeling."

"You like living in Kelna?"

"I love it." The honesty of his words surprised him, as did the desire to talk, to share with someone. "We sit on the coast of the Adriatic Sea. The water is impossibly blue. Limestone cliffs, mountains, fields of olive trees. There's a sense of community, from the largest city to the smallest town, that I have yet to find elsewhere in the world." His eyes roamed over the rooftops spread out before him. "I enjoy traveling, seeing new places. But nowhere gives me the same pleasure as when I come home."

"It sounds beautiful."

She reached for the wine bottle. Nicholai picked it up and handed it to her. Her fingers brushed his. The slight graze hit him hard. Judging by the widening of her eyes and her slightly parted lips, she experienced the same spark.

"I'm going to have to add it to my travel list." Her voice was breathless, the tiniest hint of a blush stealing across her cheeks as she looked away and sipped from the bottle.

The desire to tell her who he was, to invite her to visit him in Kelna, was so sudden and fierce he almost said it out loud. This might actually be the first time he had had a conversation with a woman simply because he wanted to talk to her. To spend time with her. Yes, there was an attraction there. Madeline was a beautiful woman.

But there was something else, something deeper pulsing beneath the initial spark. He wanted to explore it, to get to know her more. To continue the fantasy this evening had provided. One where he was a man enjoying his evening in Paris with a fascinating woman who had no designs on his title or his wealth.

For what?

He would sit on the throne in less than a year with a queen by his side. A queen he most likely hadn't even met yet. The last time he'd seen the list compiled by the prime minister's task force, he had recognized names. But he couldn't even summon the faces to go with them. He had no right to explore any type of romantic interest with another woman. He couldn't offer them anything at this point aside from a night or two of intimacy. Some men would thoroughly enjoy such an arrangement. He wasn't one of them.

Unnerved, he stood. This woman interested him more than anyone or anything had in a very long time. He needed distance. Now. Before he did something he regretted.

"It's getting late."

Madeline glanced down at her watch. Her eyes widened.

"Did we really just talk for over an hour?" She

shook her head. "I was enjoying our conversation so much I didn't even realize how long it had been."

Me, too.

For one idyllic moment, he entertained the dream of what it would be like to be normal. To ask Madeline to meet him in the morning for coffee, to explore the Louvre and travel to the top of the Eiffel Tower. To enjoy her company without wondering if paparazzi were lurking around the next corner.

The illusion vanished as quickly as it had appeared. He wasn't just a civilian. He would be fortunate if this little impromptu encounter with a random American wasn't splashed all over the tabloids by tomorrow morning.

"I'm sorry." He cooled his tone. "I have an early meeting. Otherwise, I'd stay."

He saw the flash of hurt, the smoothing of her face as she saw right through his excuse. Meeting or not, he was pushing her away, and she knew it.

"Of course." Her tiny, sweet smile nearly killed him.

She leaned over and picked up the sketch pad at her feet. Her fingers grabbed the bottom of her drawing and, before he could say anything, tugged. The penciled illustration of the Eiffel Tower tore free.

"Here."

He stared at the drawing, then back at her.

"For me?"

"Yes." Her eyes crinkled at the corners. "Something to remember Paris by when you go back home."

"I can't—"

"Yes, you can." She pressed the drawing into his hands before flipping through the sketches in the book. Images of Sacré-Coeur's elegant domes, vine-covered shops in Montmartre and the book-filled windows of Shakespeare and Company flew past. "I have plenty. I want you to have this. Please."

The *please* did him in. He nodded, unable to express his gratitude with words for fear he'd say something else, like telling her he wanted to see her again.

Let her go.

She grabbed the empty wine bottle and walked past him, a heady, sweet scent lingering in her wake. Angry with himself and, for the first time in a long time, the role he was bound to, he followed.

She moved toward a door in the wall marked *Escaliers*, tossing the wine bottle into a refuse bin by the door. They both reached for the handle. Their hands brushed. Her sharp intake of breath pierced his armor. He looked down to see her face tilted up, eyes wide and lips parted, her blonde hair glowing in the moonlight. She watched him without guile, without assessment. She simply looked at him as a woman looked at a man she desired.

He couldn't have stopped himself if he'd tried. He leaned down and kissed her.

Madeline's brain slammed to a halt even as her pulse kicked into overdrive. Nick was kissing her. And not just kissing her, but doing a very good job of it. His lips firmed on hers as he slid an arm around her waist and pulled her against him.

She should resist, her rational mind screamed at her.

But where's the adventure in that? her heart whispered back.

She gave in to temptation and twined her arms around his neck, pulling him closer. He groaned, his hands flattening against her back, warmth seeping in through her shirt. When his tongue teased the seam of her lips, she smiled and opened her mouth to him.

Her fingers crept up into the thick silkiness of his hair. Every touch was heightened, every sound amplified as they kissed, exploring each other with excited yet gentle touches, the sweetness of discovery mixing with the illicitness of a rooftop rendezvous. Whether it was the magic of their surroundings or simply the heady masculinity of the man kissing her like he was starving—even as he cradled her like the most precious of jewels—she'd never experienced a kiss like it before.

One hand drifted up into her hair, fingers tangling in her curls as he anchored her head in a firm grip and trailed his lips across her cheek. Warmth bloomed in her chest.

He pulled back, keeping one hand in her hair, the other pressed against her back. He lowered his forehead to hers, a gesture that somehow seemed more intimate than the kiss they had just shared. Their labored breathing mingled in the night air.

She raised her head, something twisting in her chest at the regret in his eyes.

Tension gripped her. "You're not married, are you?"

He let out a quiet chuckle. "No."

"Girlfriend?"

"No girlfriend, no fiancée, no wife."

She relaxed and let out a breath. "Okay."

He pulled her closer for one long, blissful moment, then released her and stepped back, her drawing now wrinkled but still clutched in his hand.

"But I'm not free to pursue this." He looked out toward the darkened spire of the tower. "No matter how much I want to."

Disappointment and the all-too-familiar bite of rejection rose up before she squelched it. She'd just met him. They'd talked for a while and, yes, shared the sweetest kiss she'd ever experienced. But she would not lose sleep over a man who was setting a very clear boundary.

"It's all right," she said with what she hoped was a casual smile. "Thank you for my adventure."

His gaze swung back to her and he frowned. "Your adventure?"

"I promised myself I'd have an adventure in Paris, and this definitely counts as one." She gestured toward the balcony. "But next time, Superman, use the stairs."

With that final pronouncement, she opened the door to the stairwell and descended. She made it back to her room, closing the door and locking it behind her before sinking down onto the bed. Her room, tucked into a corner, offered her a simple street view.

Slowly, she sucked in a shuddering breath, then released it. Her hand drifted up, her fingers settling on her swollen lips, physical evidence that she hadn't just imagined her too-handsome would-be rescuer.

She flopped back on the bed and stared up at the ceiling. She'd dated before, had had a couple boyfriends here and there. And then Alex, of course.

And look at how well that turned out, she thought cynically.

But none of them, including the early days with Alex before he'd revealed his misogynistic malarkey, had come close to inspiring the kind of sensations Nick had with one simple kiss.

With a deep inhale, she sat back up and moved

to the shower, turning the water to blistering hot. Yes, it had hurt when he'd stepped back. But, she reminded herself as she stepped under the scalding spray, she wasn't interested in relationships anyway. Not for a while, at least. Not after Alex, less than a month into their engagement, had delivered his ultimatum that she find another job when they got married or he'd call off the wedding. Alex had loved that he was dating an architect, name-dropping her job title anytime they went out to one of the many parties he'd liked to attend as an up-and-coming lawyer with a prestigious firm in Kansas City. What he hadn't loved were the long hours when she was on a demanding project and couldn't go to one of said parties, or how her career soared while his stayed stagnant.

Anger slithered through her. In the early days of their dating, she'd told him how important her career was to her. How the hours she'd spent with her stepfather, watching him draft plans for airports, courthouses and skyscrapers had led to her passion for architecture. How, after his death, it had been a way to keep his memory alive.

At first, she'd thought Alex asking to spend more time together was romantic, that he couldn't bear the thought of them being apart. But it had been control, not love, that had dictated his words. Just like it had been control that had led to their last fight, when he'd once again asked when she was quitting her job.

"I've told you how important my career is to me," she'd said as he'd stood in the living room of her apartment, hands in his pockets, shoulders thrown back in an arrogant stance as he looked down his nose at her.

"Yes, I know, you loved drawing as a kid, you spent time with your stepdad, blah, blah, blah," Alex had said with a scoff. "Stop living in the past, Maddie. What's more important? His memory or a life with me?"

She'd been wringing her hands, wondering if leaving Alex was the best thing, if he hadn't been partially right about her obsession with her career. But once he'd asked that question, the answer had been so clear and so strong it had been an easy matter to slide the diamond ring off her finger as she'd walked over to him, dropped it in his hand and told him to get out of her apartment.

Alex had been a controlling, narcissistic jerk. And she'd ignored the warning signs until it was almost too late.

Don't think about him, she ordered herself as she washed her hair.

She had just spent an hour on a rooftop in Paris with a handsome, mysterious stranger. She'd experienced the most wonderful kiss of her life… so far. And instead of mourning what might have been, on bad days she'd be able to look back at this night and spin dreams about who the enigmatic

Nick was. A foreign spy, a technology billionaire, a prince in disguise.

Cheered by her wild imagination, she stepped out of the shower. Tomorrow she would meet with J.T. and the rest of the team from Forge Architecture and find out what the top-secret assignment was. One day she would make time to date, to fall in love, get married and have a family. For now, though, her career, her family and her friends were more than enough. They'd become even more important as she'd carved out a life for herself in the aftermath of her broken engagement. Unlike Alex, her loved ones gave her room to breathe and supported her dreams. Her career offered independence and, now, the chance to travel.

She definitely didn't need another relationship tying her down now.

But as she lay down, Nick's handsome face crossed her mind. She couldn't suppress the question that arose as she drifted off to sleep.

What if...?

CHAPTER THREE

MADELINE WRAPPED HER hands around her mug of tea and relaxed in her chair as the morning sounds of Paris washed over her. Birds tweeted overheard. Soft music played quietly from speakers hidden in urns overflowing with vivid pink blooms. On the other side of the stone wall, car engines purred as the occasional horn beeped. Her sketch pad lay nearby. After her cup of tea, she'd draw the courtyard before her team arrived. Another memory to take home.

She glanced at the glossy black leather binding. Buried toward the back was a sketch she'd done this morning as the buildings of Paris had turned to rose in the dawn light. A strong blade of a nose. A long, handsome face marked by a square jaw with a dimple in the middle and a reluctant smile tilting up one corner of full lips.

And the eyes...the eyes had been the hardest. She'd drawn, erased, drawn again, then finally settled for the best she could do. Nothing would capture the brooding intensity, the hidden depths that had slowly flickered to life the longer they'd talked.

She sighed. Nick had quickly turned from an unwanted intruder to, so far at least, her best memory of Paris.

So far.

It would be hard to make a better memory. But she still had all of today and the promise of tomorrow. Still had a mystery that her boss, J.T., would unveil within the hour. Content with her thoughts, she settled deeper into her chair. A week ago, she never would have imagined herself sitting at a table laden with breads, jams, fruit and juices spread out on a neat white tablecloth with the spire of the Eiffel Tower visible in the distance.

She loved her job.

"Oh, my God."

Madeline looked up to see Julie, Andrew and Chris walk into the courtyard. Julie's and Andrew's eyes were round as saucers as they took in the tiered fountain splashing off to the side, the cobblestone pavers and the leafy trees arching overheard.

Chris shot her a megawatt smile. She suppressed a groan and gave him a polite smile in return. A few years older than her, Chris, with his sunstreaked blond hair, lanky build and skin tanned to gold thanks to hours spent outside, appealed to a lot of women. He'd hinted more than once at getting together for an after-work drink. But she didn't mix work with relationships. That rule extended to coworkers and clients. Perhaps she was being overly proper, but it wasn't worth the risk.

No relationship was right now. Not after she'd been so spectacularly wrong about Alex and got sucked into his self-centered world. She had always considered herself a good judge of character. Had she let the idea of being in a relationship, of moving on to steps like marriage and kids, blind her to the warning signs of who Alex was beneath his handsome charm?

She frowned. She hadn't thought this much about Alex in nearly six months. It had been well over a year since she'd kicked him out. She'd been content to focus on her career, enjoy time with her family and friends. What had brought this on?

Him.

The answer appeared before she'd even fully formed the question in her mind. Nick had been the first man she'd felt something for in a very long time. But her attraction to him had also brought her fears to the surface.

A good sign, she told herself firmly as she greeted her colleagues, *that you're not ready for any kind of dating.*

"Good! You're all here," a voice boomed across the courtyard.

James Theodore Sanderson, affectionately known as J.T., walked out of the double glass doors as if he were making an entrance onto a stage. With an old-fashioned moustache the color of steel gracing his upper lip, the ends curled into extravagant flourishes, and thick jowls that descended into an even thicker neck, J.T. reminded her of a bulldog with a never-ending smile. He'd been like that ever since the year he'd guest lectured in one of her college classes, offering her first an internship and then a job at his firm once she'd passed her exams. While no one could ever replace her stepfather, J.T. had been both a mentor and a paternal figure in her life.

He slapped his hands together and beamed at them. "Are you ready, *mes petits enfants*?"

Julie, a curvy woman in her forties with a quick smile and a brunette bob that framed her round face, arched a brow. "For?"

"The reveal."

Madeline couldn't help but laugh. "You're practically shaking, you're so excited. I've never seen you like this over a contract before."

"It's a big one."

A buzz hummed through Madeline's veins. In the five years she'd been working for Forge, three as an intern and two as a fully licensed architect, she'd fallen in love with each and every project she'd tackled. J.T. loved his work, too. But after forty years in the business, including thirty running his own firm, little got him this excited. It had to be something big.

"Our client is on his way down to meet with us. I have your nondisclosure agreements on file." J.T.

sobered, the twinkle disappearing from his eye as he leaned forward and speared them with an intense gaze. "Not a word of this project, nor who we're working for, must be shared with anyone, including your families. Not until we receive approval from his public relations team."

Andrew, a former university classmate of hers with a stocky build and thick beard, rolled his eyes, the gesture magnified by his oversize glasses.

"We signed the paperwork, J.T. Either you trust us or you don't."

J.T. held up his hands. "Fair." His eyes shifted and a smile spread across his face.

"Ah, Your Highness! I was just briefing my team."

Julie's eyes grew round as she mouthed, "Your Highness?"

Excitement skittered through Madeline. They'd worked with business leaders and politicians and even a couple of local celebrities, but never a member of royalty.

"Please, Mr. Sanderson, there's no need for formalities."

Madeline froze. She knew that voice, smooth whiskey roughened by that sexy accent.

This isn't happening.

Slowly, she turned her head.

He dominated the courtyard with his presence. Navy suit, complete with a crisp white shirt and silver tie, screamed custom tailoring and money.

His dark hair had been tamed back from his forehead, the chiseled planes and angles of his striking face on display for all to see.

Their eyes connected. Did she imagine the flicker of recognition, followed by something darker? Or did he truly not recognize her?

She wasn't sure which was worse.

"Team, this is His Royal Highness, Prince Nicholai Adamović of Kelna. His father, King Ivan Adamović, is an old friend of mine."

Oh, my God, I kissed a prince.

Everyone stood and introductions were made, J.T. announcing everyone's names and titles like a proud father introducing his children.

"And this is Madeline, one of my best design architects."

"Your Highness." She bobbed in place, keeping one hand wrapped tightly around the back of her chair.

Nick—no, Prince Nicholai—inclined his head, the same as he had to the others. His professional demeanor took the edge off the panic fluttering around in her stomach.

Okay.

She released a breath. She could pretend like last night had never happened, too. Even if it stung that he was able to pass off their conversation and kiss so easily.

"I look forward to working with you."

He nodded to her, then turned back to J.T. She

swallowed hard and glanced up at the tip of the Eiffel Tower. Had it been less than ten hours ago that she had admired it with the man standing just feet away? A man who had listened to her, shared pieces of himself, then kissed her like she was the most precious thing in the world.

A man who had just now dismissed her as if they had never met.

Stop it.

As heroic and intriguing as he'd seemed last night, his cool dismissal made it clear that that's all it had been: one night. If she was going to maintain her professional role, the only option she had was to remove herself from her emotions and do her job.

Nicholai sat at the head of the table, and they all sank back into their chairs.

"Have you shared the details of the project yet, Mr. Sanderson?"

Nicholai's voice commanded everyone's attention, low and deep.

"Not yet. Would you care to do the honors, Your Highness?"

"Nicholai, please," the Prince said with a wave of his hand. "Titles and formal addresses are for government functions and black-tie events." He glanced around the table, his eyes landing on each member of the team. Madeline could swear she heard Julie let out a deep sigh, a noise that made her lips twitch, given that Julie had been happily married for nearly twenty years.

And then Nicholai's gaze landed on her. The air disappeared from her lungs, leaving her chest tight and her skin warm. Something flickered in his eyes—something dark—then disappeared as he continued his perusal of the table.

"My father, King Ivan Adamović, rules Kelna. It's a small country slivered between Croatia and Montenegro. Mountains, fields and a small stretch of coastline along the Adriatic Sea. Our country has a population of less than five hundred thousand. But our economy is strong, primarily powered by tourism along our coast. That's about to change with the addition of a new seaport that will allow us to serve close to three thousand ships a year."

His expression didn't change. But his voice deepened, the pride in his country's accomplishments evident despite the professional veneer that kept his handsome features smooth.

"We've experienced an influx of money from those who want to see the port succeed, enough that we've been able to advance projects like the building of new highways, railway repair, new schools and other projects." His smile flashed, cool but no less potent. "With the rise in interest, we'll be hosting more official visits to our palace. A palace that has not been updated in forty years. That's where your team comes in."

Excitement chased away some of Madeline's tension.

"The palace is a conglomeration of Roman and European styles. It started off as a fortress along the coast, similar to Diocletian's Palace in Croatia. Many of the rooms have been updated over the years. But some, like our ballroom, saw little use. Until now, money was not something our country had a great deal of to spend on vanity projects. Other than the necessary maintenance, rooms like the ballroom are like time capsules from various eras. The Napoleonic Wars, the Industrial Revolution." His lips twisted into a wry smirk. "The result is certainly…interesting."

"Eclectic," Julie offered.

"A kind way to put it," Nicholai said with a smile. "While we don't want to destroy the history of the palace, we do need to bring these rooms into the twenty-first century. Our first project is the grand ballroom." He gestured to J.T. "We've arranged for your team to fly out tomorrow morning for an initial meeting to review the code and zoning analyses already conducted by members of our team and to discuss details. Then we'll tour the original ballroom, the site for the new one, and, if time allows, the highlights of our palace before flying you all home the next day. We'll reconvene four weeks later to view your initial designs."

Madeline's eyebrows raised as she shot a look

at J.T. They had never completed a design for a project in a matter of weeks. Had J.T. actually agreed to this?

"Is there a problem, Miss Delvine?"

Madeline's head swung around. Nicholai stared at her, the silkiness of his voice contrasting sharply with the emotion seething in his eyes. An emotion that looked uncomfortably like repugnance.

Was he upset that she had left so abruptly last night? Or was he irritated that the woman he had indiscreetly kissed was going to be in his life for the foreseeable future?

She raised her chin. Prince or no prince, the man was not going to bully her.

"I have concerns about the timeline, that's all. The predesign phase alone can take a month, and developing schematic drawings another month to two. However," she added with a nod to her boss, "I imagine J.T. has something in mind. He wouldn't have accepted the project otherwise."

"Quite right," J.T. said in his booming voice. "It is a tight timeline. The progress check-in isn't for a final delivery, just to present the schematics and a couple artistic renderings to the royal family. From there it will go to a community panel. King Ivan wants the country to be a part of the process and emphasize that the ballroom will be used for a variety of events, including ones for the people of Kelna." J.T. shot a smile at Madeline. "I appreciate you asking, Maddie."

She sat back. Even though she admired the King's including his people in the decision-making process, the accelerated timeline still made her uncomfortable. But she trusted J.T. If he said he thought it was possible, then it was. He wouldn't risk the reputation of Forge in committing to something he couldn't do, not even for an old friend.

J.T. passed out a folder containing pictures of the palace. Despite the plethora of styles, from the pervading Roman grandeur to the touches of ornate Gothic and classic Renaissance influences, the palace was stunning. Limestone walls gleamed like diamonds in the aerial shots, brilliant white made all the more dramatic by the blue sea a stone's throw away. Many of the rooms still proudly boasted their elegant history with soaring ceilings, marble pillars and intricate stained glass windows. Coupled with the modern touches that had been introduced over the past few decades, it was a lovely and unique structure.

The current ballroom, however, made her wince. A long, thin room, it looked like something from a British country manor. The ornate crown molding, while beautifully carved, seemed ostentatious and overwhelming coupled with the low ceilings. Chandeliers dripping in crystals shrank the room even further. It seemed as if someone had ignored the adage "less is more" and stuffed every possible thing they could into this room.

The next photos, however, made her sit up. The site that had been marked for the new ballroom took her breath away. A grassy expanse sat next to the existing ballroom. Beyond the green, pine trees flanked a clifftop that plunged down into the sea. A stunning garden was visible in the distance. As she flipped through the photos, designs etched themselves in her mind.

Her earlier excitement returned. This, she felt in her bones, was going to be an incredible project.

"Given how busy tomorrow is going to be," J.T. said, "you have the rest of the day to yourselves. We'll meet in the lobby tomorrow morning at 7:00 a.m. for our flight."

Madeline quickly stood. Perhaps she was imagining the tension between her and Nicholai. But real or not, she wanted to get as far away from it as possible.

"It was nice to meet you, Your Highness," she said with a quick bob. She scooped up her folder and headed toward the door.

Run up to the room. Jot down some of these ideas. Then stroll down the Champs-élysées and pretend like I can afford—

"Where are you headed to?"

She inwardly groaned as Chris fell into step beside her.

"I'm not sure. I had a couple ideas I wanted to write down. Then maybe go out for a walk. What about you?"

"I'm headed to the Musée d'Art Moderne. You should join me."

He flashed her a smile and she knew a moment of frustration. Why couldn't she be attracted to someone like Chris? Someone who was interested in her, who shared her passion for architecture?

But no matter how hard she tried, she couldn't summon anything more than feelings of friendship.

"You could bring your sketch pad," he added with a nod to the book in her hands. "Show Matisse and Picasso a thing or two."

The comment teased a genuine smile from her. "How about I text you after lunch, see where you're at?"

His face fell, but he nodded. "Sure."

They entered the cool interior of the hotel. Chris headed toward the front door while Madeline walked to the elevator, her mind almost immediately returning to the man just a few dozen feet behind her.

A prince. She had kissed a prince. One day she would tell her mom and her siblings, maybe even Julie. One day, it would be one of those moments she looked back on with fondness and a dash of excitement.

But right now, it was just frustrating. How was she supposed to work for someone who had gone from talking with her on a rooftop and kissing her senseless to acting like she was worse than the dirt on his shoes?

They'd have to talk, she acknowledged glumly as she pressed the elevator button. Clear the air. Even though he had already drawn the line last night on their little tête-à-tête going any further, his being a client was more than enough incentive for her to keep her distance. She would never risk her career for a fling. She would reassure him of that, reiterate her commitment to the job. Hopefully, that would be enough.

The elevator doors slid open. She stepped inside and pushed the button for the third floor. The doors started to close when a hand shot out. A small alarm beeped and they slid open to reveal a stone-faced Prince Nicholai Adamović.

"Going up alone?"

She frowned at his frigid tone.

"Unless there's a ghost lurking in here with me, yes."

"I didn't know if you were waiting for Chris."

Frustration pumped through her as she narrowed her eyes. "You're my client. That entitles you to know my professional background, skills and what I'm doing with your project. It does not give you the right to know who I choose to spend time with."

The elevator door started to beep more incessantly. Nicholai stepped inside. The doors closed, leaving them alone.

She knew it was impossible for spatial relationships to change. But her brain insisted that the elevator shrank because suddenly it seemed like no matter where she moved, she would be inches away from touching the Prince.

"How did you arrange it?"

Her brows drew together.

"What?"

"Last night. What was your plan? Draw me out, have a photographer waiting to capture us?" He leaned down, the gold flecks in his eyes a vivid flash against dark green. "Were you trying to trick me into a compromising position, or perhaps have some gossip to sell to a magazine?"

"'A compromising position,'" she echoed. "Did you steal my copy of *Pride and Prejudice*? This isn't the Regency era. A man and a woman are allowed to have a private conversation without being engaged or married."

He looked away and ran a hand through his hair, muttering something in a deep, guttural language that stirred the air and, despite her irritation, made her heart beat a little faster.

"It's not the same for someone like me."

"Okay," she said slowly. "Look, I know neither of us expected to see each other again. But I want to reassure you that I—"

"Are you sure you never intended to see me again?" The venom in his voice put her on high alert as he pinned her in place with his gaze. "Or did you know who I was all along? Did you decide to sneak up onto that roof with the hope of capturing my attention?"

Irritation burst into righteous anger. She tried, and failed, to swallow the words that rose up.

"One, you will never speak to me in that tone again. Understand?"

Nicholai blinked. "Excuse me?"

"You're a prince. Congratulations. That doesn't give you the right to talk to me like I'm trash. Second, do you really think last night was a setup?" She cocked her head to the side. "I mean, it makes perfect sense to me. I went up on the roof of the hotel my boss booked for me a week ago, to a spot that was out of the line of sight of your room, on the tiny whim that you might go to the window and look off to the side? Oh, and that you," she said with a stab of her finger in his general direction, "would develop a superhero complex and jump off of a balcony to rescue me?"

His brows drew together.

"Surely even you have to see how—"

"Even me? A lowly commoner? No, apparently, I'm too simple to see how any rational human being could picture last night being a setup."

The elevator dinged. The doors slid open and she brushed past him.

"Madeline."

The sound of her name, uttered in that husky accent, slid over her. Heat pricked her eyes as she remembered how he'd said her name last night, of how special she'd felt under the magic of a Parisian sky.

She whipped around. He stood in the door of the elevator, one arm braced against the frame, a thunderous expression on his face.

"Don't worry. I'm going to pretend like last night never happened. As far as you and I are concerned, we met for the first time this morning. I won't say anything to anyone, including my team, reporters or anyone else you're concerned might find out. If you can treat me with slightly more respect and politeness, then we'll get along just fine."

He sighed and scrubbed a hand over his jaw.

"Madeline—"

"Have a good day." She punched the button to close the door, grateful when he stepped back.

And couldn't resist one last parting shot. She grasped her skirt in her hands and dropped into a deep curtsy as the doors started to slide shut. "Your Highness."

CHAPTER FOUR

"LUNCH IS SERVED."

Nicholai looked up as Marina, the head flight attendant, set a plate on the table in front of him. The familiar savory scent of cuttlefish and risotto relaxed the tension that had gripped him since yesterday morning.

The team had arrived a half hour before their departure time. J.T., Julie, Andrew and Chris had been excited at riding on the private jet chartered by the palace. The plane had been divided into three sections, with the first dedicated mostly to crew space and a guest bathroom. The primary section, the main cabin, boasted a mix of luxurious ivory leather chairs, a sofa at the front and one at the back and a long table the same gleaming black wood as the floors. The back of the plane included a private suite with a bed, shower and walk-in closet. Even if it was more ostentatious than Nicholai preferred, he appreciated the intimate setting.

The luxury hadn't seemed to faze Madeline one

bit as she'd given him a brief nod, glanced around the plane, and then moved as far away from him as she could get.

His eyes strayed toward the back of the plane. Madeline sat in one of the plush chairs with her legs curled under her. With her blond hair pulled into a messy bun on top of her head and a pair of round glasses, she looked more like a college student than an architect as she sketched.

Watching her hand fly over the paper made him remember the drawing tucked safely in his briefcase. A drawing he'd pulled out at least twice since she'd given it to him. Once, when he'd awoken the morning after to an ache in his chest that had plagued him until the moment he'd walked into the courtyard and seen Madeline's beautiful face frozen in surprise. An ache replaced by a thrilling jolt, then squelched by anger as he'd fought to make it through the meeting without demanding answers.

The second time had been after she'd left him speechless in the elevator. He'd smoothed the crinkles left in the paper from when he'd crushed the drawing against her back as he'd kissed her. The light of day had shown him the details he'd missed in the night: the rivets climbing up the side of the tower, the intricate latticework, even the detailing on the bridge where the couple stood, spoke to her talent, both as an artist and as an architect.

A breath escaped him. Franjo's betrayal had

made him distrustful. Madeline had paid the price for his irrational suspicions. For someone who usually held himself to the pillars of honor and duty, he'd screwed up. Royally.

Chris crouched down next to her chair and murmured something. Madeline looked up and blinked owlishly. She glanced over at the table, watched Marina set more plates down, then shook her head with a small smile. Nicholai's fingers tightened around his pen as whatever Chris said next teased a laugh from her. When he patted her on the knee as he stood, Nicholai nearly snapped his pen in half.

He'd seen the way the architect had looked at Madeline at the hotel, had overheard his invitation to explore around the museum. He couldn't remember the last time he had ever wished someone would trip over their own feet or walk into a window.

But he had entertained numerous thoughts of that nature in the past twenty-four hours about Chris.

The younger man looked up and caught Nicholai's gaze. His expression faltered. Inwardly cursing, Nicholai forced a slight smile and nodded before turning his attention to the dish in front of him.

"This looks great." Andrew grinned, his teeth white against his dark brown skin as he took the seat next to Nicholai's. "Seafood?"

"Cuttlefish. Known as *crni rižot* in Croatia."

"It smells amazing." Julie, the project architect, took her seat next to Andrew. "I've never had black risotto before."

"The color comes from squid ink."

Julie blanched. "Oh."

Nicholai smiled at her. "I promise it's worth a taste. But the crew can prepare something else."

Julie sighed and picked up her fork. "I'm always getting on to my kids about trying new food. Can't do that if I don't practice what I preach." She scooped up a forkful and paused, scrunching her eyes before she took a bite. Her eyes flew open. "Oh, wow. Wow, this is really good. Maddie!"

Madeline's head jerked up. Her eyes flickered to Nicholai, then to Julie.

"Maddie, you are missing out!"

"I'll have some later." Madeline nodded toward the pad in her lap. "I'm on a roll here."

"Madeline is very good at design work," Julie confided as she dug into her dish. "So is Chris."

Chris smiled and shrugged. "I'm decent. Madeline's the true talent on the team."

Nicholai gave him a thin-lipped smile in return. Even the man's humbleness grated on his nerves.

"I'm not familiar with the different roles you all play."

"So I'm the project architect—"

"Big boss," Andrew clarified as he slathered butter on a thick slice of *pogača* bread.

"Big boss," Julie agreed with a grin. "Andrew is our site architect. He's the one who makes our lovely pictures come to life. J.T., of course," she said with a nod toward the back where J.T. dozed, "handles all the administrative things, although he used to be a legendary designer himself. And then Chris and Madeline are the design architects."

As Julie rattled off the details of all the roles she had just mentioned, Nicholai tried to listen. Tried to focus on what would be not only an important project, but one that carried a lot of pride for the people of Kelna. After centuries of being forgotten, they were finally being recognized for the incredible country they'd created and sustained over generations.

Yet his eyes kept straying back to Madeline. How she chewed on the tip of her pen or tapped it against the paper in her lap when she was puzzled. How at one point she glanced at everyone seated at the round table and, thinking no one was watching, pushed off the wall with her foot and spun in a circle.

His lips curved up.

"So what do you think?"

Nicholai froze.

"I'm not sure." He shook his head and smiled at Julie. "I apologize. I tuned out for the last part of our conversation. Could you repeat the question?"

Julie waved her hand. "Just me jumping ahead

to business. I'm sorry. I'm just so excited to get to work."

This time, the smile Nicholai gave Julie was reassuring. "No need to apologize. I'm honored to work with a team as excited about this project as I am. It's why my father wanted to work with J.T.'s firm."

"Thank you, Your Highness."

"Nicholai," he gently prodded her. "Now, you mentioned children. How many do you have?"

Julie's cheeks turned pink with pleasure. "Three. Two boys and a girl…"

As Julie spoke, awareness sparked across Nicholai's skin. He looked up, saw Madeline watching him, a furrow between her brows. Pink swept over her cheeks when their eyes connected. She hurriedly glanced back down at the papers in her lap.

Unreasonably pleased at her reaction, he refocused on Julie and her stories about her children. Andrew and Chris chipped in with tales like when Julie's daughter had let the family's new puppy loose in J.T.'s office during an important client meeting. The rest of the flight passed in casual conversation, with the team sharing everything from how they got started in architecture to their favorite places in Kansas City.

Nicholai leaned back in his chair. His father had chosen well. He liked J.T.'s team, even if he didn't want to like Chris. They were talented and worked well together. The personal touch they brought, the camaraderie, all of it spoke well for the work they were about to do.

"Ladies and gentlemen, *dames i gospodo*, we are beginning our initial descent into Kelna."

The pilot, Nada, spoke smoothly over the speaker.

"Oh!"

The simple breathless syllable made Nicholai look up. Madeline had moved to a window and now had her hands pressed to the glass like an excited child. He got up from the table and made his way back to her.

"What do you think?"

"It's like looking down on a…a…"

"Fairy-tale kingdom?"

She glanced up at him, her eyes slightly narrowed. When she saw the small smile hovering about his lips, she grinned in return, an uninhibited gesture that made his chest tighten.

"Exactly."

She turned back to the window and he followed her stare. The deep blue waters of the Adriatic Sea lightened into shades of aquamarine as they neared the coast. A beach covered with golden sand hugged a promenade that stretched the length of the town behind it. Lepa Plavi stood in its proud, historic splendor beyond the beach. Buildings of pale stone were made vivid by their red-tiled roofs. As the plane drew closer, the narrow, winding streets became visible, along with the bustle of people visiting the markets, shops and restaurants.

And to the left, on a hilltop overlooking the sea, stood the Palace of Kelna. The limestone walls gleamed like a jewel in the afternoon sun, with over a thousand years of history residing in its ivory-colored walls.

"How do you ever leave here?"

"It's hard." He nodded toward the mountains in the distance, the green hills sloping up to thick pine forests that covered all but the snowcapped tops of Kelna's majestic peaks. "My country has something for everyone. The entrepreneur, the family, the explorer." His eyes roved over the familiar sights beneath him before straying to a site just beyond the wingtip of the plane. A site that had changed drastically in such a short amount of time. "Now for the industrialist, too."

"You're not certain about that."

Surprised, he looked down at her.

"What makes you say that?"

One shoulder rose and fell. "You hesitated."

Slowly, he released a deep breath. "This port will bring great prosperity to our country. But also, great change."

"Change can be good."

"Yes."

His eyes returned to the site of the new port. Massive cranes stood against the backdrop of the sky, mechanical and out of place next to Lepa Plavi's mix of Roman and European architecture.

"But how does one know when there is too much change?"

Madeline tried to keep her ears tuned to the guide escorting them through the winding hallways.

And failed miserably.

Marble dominated the palace, from the gleaming floors to soaring pillars. Over two hundred rooms made up the complex. The palace library boasted two floors of books, complete with dark walnut bookcases and actual sliding ladders. From the vaulted ceilings painted with elaborate designs in the grand hall where official guests were welcomed to the more solemn yet still elegant columns that marched down the art gallery, it was magnificent.

The ballroom was another story, and just as over-the-top as it had appeared in the photos. Whereas rooms like the Hall of Mirrors at Versailles exuded historical charm, this looked like it had been done purely to show how much money the old King had had to waste. Andrew scribbled note after note on his tablet.

The project was massive.

She couldn't wait to get started.

They passed by the large bay windows of a room that overlooked one of the numerous gardens. Her eyes roamed over the stone paths that meandered through lush lotus plants, colorful orchids and acacia trees.

Had Nicholai played here as a child? Explored the paths and pretended he was a pirate or a wizard? Or had he been studious, focused, even as a youngster?

Irritated with herself, she quickened her pace to catch up to the group. She'd managed to hold on to her indignation from his ridiculous accusations all the way onto the plane. Even when she'd caught him looking at her, she'd ignored him.

Until he'd been kind and talked to Julie, shown genuine interest in her colleagues. Until he'd looked down at the shores of his homeland and spoken with both pride and the gravity of someone who understood the depth of his responsibility and duty.

She blew a stray hair out of her face. She didn't want to like him. Didn't want to think about his good qualities, which would inevitably lead her back to that night in Paris.

Focus on your work! Not a prince who is completely off-limits.

A prince who had thankfully seen them off in two small limos at the airport before departing in his own. He'd met them on the front steps of the palace, where an aide had escorted them to a charming conference room overlooking well-tended gardens. The meeting was quick and effective. Members of the survey team, along with people from departments like finance and public affairs, had met to review the detailed reports. It had been one of the most prepared client sessions Madeline had ever attended. She'd even managed to keep her mind on their work.

Mostly.

Except for when Nicholai had laughed at something Andrew had said. The deep sound, a moment of relaxed amusement, had slid over her and made her breath catch. Or when she'd caught him nodding appreciatively to some of the questions she asked. When he had excused himself before the tour had started, she'd been equally relieved and disappointed.

The guide turned into a room that looked like a formal living room. The elegant furnishings stood out against the pale blue walls that added a touch of calm to the affluent setting.

"We've arranged for you to have some refreshments before you're shown to your rooms." Goran, a slender man with a silver mane of hair and a calming smile, gestured to a sideboard table laden with water pitchers, glasses of champagne and an array of fruits and cheeses. "Please, enjoy yourselves, take all the time you want and notify me when you're ready."

"I'm ready!" Julie said with a laugh. "I haven't walked this much in a long time."

J.T. echoed her sentiment. Goran led them out

one of the doors, leaving Madeline alone with Andrew and Chris.

Andrew sank down into a chair and continued to scribble furiously. Chris picked up two glasses of champagne and handed one to Madeline.

"This is incredible."

"It is." Madeline's eyes roamed over the rectangular room, drank in the sight of rounded bay windows offset by elaborate columns, the marble fireplace at the far end. "I wish we could stay longer. Twenty-four hours isn't nearly enough."

"We'll be back in four weeks." Chris nodded in Andrew's direction. "Andrew's already got all the blueprints and a crew coming through later this week to take photos. We'll have everything we need."

"True." She wrinkled her nose. "Not a fan of the accelerated timeline."

"At least it'll be a challenge," Chris said as he clinked his glass to hers.

"True." She sipped the champagne, enjoyed the dance of bubbles on her tongue.

"Never one to back down." Chris smiled at her. "I like that about you."

Some of Madeline's joy disappeared. She inwardly groaned. She didn't want to hurt him. But her more passive approach had done nothing to discourage him. She liked Chris, appreciated him as a work partner and as a friend. She didn't want to lose that, especially with the largest project of their careers on the line.

"Chris—"

"Miss Delvine."

Nicholai's voice swept over her. Chris frowned, his gaze shifting from her face to the Prince behind her.

Swallowing hard, she turned and dipped her head. "Your Highness."

"May I have a word?"

Her heart kicked up its pace.

"Of course, sir." She glanced over her shoulder at Chris, shrugged to show him she didn't know what Nicholai wanted and followed Nicholai out into the hall. He led the way to a small alcove set amongst a pair of columns.

"Yes?"

Nicholai glanced around before pinning her with his intense gaze.

"I wanted to apologize."

She loathed that her heart gave a traitorous leap. "Apologize?"

"For my discourtesy yesterday. My accusations were thoughtless and insensitive."

She threaded her fingers together and rocked back on her heels as nerves fluttered in her belly.

"Thanks. It's okay."

"But it's not. I was rude."

"You were. But," she added with a sigh, "I wasn't exactly polite myself."

Nicholai's lips twitched. "You had just cause."

"Still, it's not the way my mom raised me to behave. Especially to a prince." She stuck out her hand. "Truce?"

"Truce."

His hand enveloped hers. Energy sparked between them, curled up her arm and flooded her with sensation. Her breath caught in her chest. Her eyes swept up, met his equally stunned gaze.

"Sir—"

"Please call me Nicholai." He blinked, as if shocked by his own request.

"Nicholai."

She repeated his name softly, saying it in its entirety for the first time. His fingers tightened around hers.

"Madeline—"

"Maddie?"

She gasped and yanked her hand away as Andrew called down the hallway. Suddenly frantic at the possibility of being caught in a secluded alcove with the man who would be signing off on her company's paychecks, she moved into the hallway.

"Yes?"

Andrew cocked his head to one side as she walked toward him.

"What were you doing?"

"Exploring," she replied with a bright smile, her stomach twisting at the lie. She barely resisted looking over her shoulder to see if Nicholai had followed. "What's up?"

"Goran is taking Chris and I up to our rooms. We didn't want to leave you behind."

"Great. I'll join you."

She followed Andrew back to the reception room. It had been a good thing, she told herself, that Andrew had interrupted whatever had been about to happen.

But it didn't stop her from pausing in the doorway and risking a discreet glance down the hall.

The hall was empty.

CHAPTER FIVE

BUTTERFLIES FLUTTERED IN Madeline's stomach as she slid a cover over the final illustration.

You've got this. You've got this.

She'd been repeating the same mantra since yesterday when she'd boarded a plane from Kansas City to Paris with Chris and Julie, followed by another private jet to Kelna. J.T. and Andrew had gone out a week early to meet with a team of civil engineers to discuss the technical details of the new ballroom.

She stepped back and surveyed the easels set up at the far end of what Goran had described as the "Ivory Room." An elegant conference room painted a creamy white that made the azure-colored waves of the Adriatic, viewed from arched windows that took up most of one wall, even more striking. A long cherrywood table dominated the middle of the room. She'd laid out enough copies of the presentation folder for the royal family and the Forge team. Everything was in order, which meant the worst part had arrived.

Waiting.

In less than thirty minutes, she and her team would present their initial plan to King Ivan, Prince Nicholai and Nicholai's sister, Princess Eviana. Designs that normally took months, but had been produced in just one.

The past four weeks had been chaotic. Ever since they'd landed back in Kansas City, they'd put in twelve-to-fifteen-hour days to meet Nicholai's demanding deadline. If the royals approved, the proposal would be submitted to a committee of citizens who would cast the final vote.

No pressure. No pressure at all.

The punishing pace had had one upside. It had kept her focus on her work and off those last, fraught seconds with Nicholai in the alcove.

Except for at night, when a glimpse of the stars from her bedroom window or a taste of wine at dinner stirred the memories she'd fought to push away.

She didn't want a relationship right now. She needed a break, time to be alone, before she dated again. Even if she was ready to date, Nicholai was the Prince of a rapidly growing European nation. She was an architect from the Midwest. Interested or not, a relationship was out of the question.

In a moment of weakness, she'd looked him up on the flight home. The sheer number of reports speculating on his love life had been overwhelming. For all the gossip and rumors, one theme had emerged: Nicholai would most likely wed in the next year as his father's health deteriorated. His future bride would be an integral part of Kelna's growth.

Madeline felt sorry for the poor woman already. To have that kind of weight resting on one's shoulders before even saying "I do"? To have a marriage rooted in strategy and policy instead of love?

No, thanks.

The tabloid speculation had also planted a seed of discomfort in her chest. Nicholai had told her there was no woman in the picture. Technically that was true. But the fact that he might be married within a year was something he'd forgotten to mention.

She sighed. The tabloids could easily be writing fiction to sell stories. And why was she pondering any of this when none of it mattered? No, he hadn't told her. But he didn't owe her an explanation. One kiss didn't entitle her to all his secrets, or him to hers.

She needed to stop ruminating and refocus her attention on her work. On the biggest presentation of her career so far, which would take place in just a few minutes.

Relax. Take a breath. Be calm. Professional.

She drifted over to the large bay windows that overlooked the sea. She leaned her forehead against the glass, much as she had the month before as the plane had descended into Kelna.

Something about the country called to her. Yes, there was the initial excitement of being in a new place. But she'd felt something deep in her bones the first time she had laid eyes on the beaches, the pine forest, the sea. A feeling reinforced by the evening she'd spent in Lepa Plavi. J.T. had treated the entire team to dinner at a local restaurant, then set them loose for a couple hours. She'd wandered the cobblestone streets and narrow passageways, navigating buildings cloaked in history. The architect in her appreciated the strength, the sheer will that had kept the town standing for over a thousand years. The romantic in her had fallen in love with the country that had stood the test of time.

Her eyes drifted back to the easels. Chris had followed her lead the past four weeks, giving her free rein over the designs, even when she had caught a raised brow or a slight frown. The royal family's direction, to design a new ballroom that would bring it in line with the palace while updating it for the twenty-first century, had been vague at best. She'd made several sketches of the large lawn where the new ballroom would go, taken numerous pictures the morning they'd flown back home. Reviewed more photos of the existing palace and some of her favorite rooms from her tour.

And come up with the design that would be unveiled in just a few minutes. Whether it achieved what the King, Prince and Princess wanted remained to be seen.

Awareness prickled over her skin. A sharp inhale brought a scent of cedar mixed with a masculinity that painted a vivid image of a handsome smile and green eyes crinkled at the corners.

"Hello."

Squaring her shoulders, Madeline turned and laced her fingers together as she faced Prince Nicholai.

"Your Highness."

He looked incredible. Dressed in a charcoal suit with a dark green tie, his hair combed back from his face, he looked every inch the austere royal. His face was smoothed into an expressionless mask that made his sharp features look more like a statue than those of a living person.

Something inside her chest twisted. She missed the carefree smile he'd given her on the rooftops of Paris, the naked emotion in his eyes when they'd met in the alcove. On those occasions, she'd seen the man behind the crown.

Now, though…now he looked distant. Unreachable. Untouchable.

For the best. No touching the handsome prince.

"How was your flight, Miss Delvine?"

"Fine, thank you."

Silence descended. The longer it grew, the more tense it became. If Madeline thought she had imagined the attraction between them, the tension spoke otherwise.

Frustrated, she abandoned her pretense of appearing calm as she ran a hand through her hair.

"Look, I know there's—"

"Hello."

A woman appeared just behind Nicholai. Madeline instantly recognized the long black hair that hung down to her waist, the pixie-like features, and the green eyes, the only feature that Princess Eviana shared with her brother.

Madeline dipped into what she hoped was a passable curtsy.

"Your Highness."

Eviana's lips tilted up into a small *Mona Lisa* smile that radiated regality. She crossed the room and held out her hand.

"You must be Madeline."

"I am."

Madeline took the offered hand, trying to mask her surprise at the faint roughness of the Princess's palms.

"My brother's told me a lot about you."

Madeline's eyes flickered to Nicholai, then back to Eviana. The Princess's smile deepened to something genuine, edged with a touch of smug satisfaction that told Madeline she had just given something away.

Alarm flared. Surely Nicholai hadn't told his sister what had happened between them in Paris. But then again, even though he was a royal, he could still share things with his siblings like the rest of the world.

"I've enjoyed getting to know him and learn more about your country."

She hoped her answer sounded professional even as her heart raced so fast it was a wonder she didn't pass out.

"Diplomatically spoken." Eviana glanced back at her brother. "We're looking forward to seeing your work today, aren't we, *braco*?"

Thankfully, the rest of the team walked in just then. More introductions were made. Nicholai and Eviana took their seats at the far end of the table. Whatever Madeline had sensed between her and Nicholai disappeared as he resumed the mantle of prince.

Which is good, she told herself as she and Chris moved to the front of the room. *Business. This is business.*

Another man entered the room. Despite his hunched shoulders and paper-thin skin, he still exuded a calming regality that spoke of power entwined with a personability she wouldn't have expected from a king. Illness had not dimmed the intelligence in King Ivan Adamović's eyes, nor robbed him of his presence as he moved forward with the assistance of a simple black cane.

Nicholai and Eviana both stood, as did Andrew, J.T. and Julie.

J.T. bowed. "Your Majesty."

Chris and Andrew followed suit, as Julie dropped into a curtsy. Madeline hastily copied Julie's gesture.

"Please." King Ivan waved a wrinkled hand as he approached J.T. "Friends do not bow to one another or address each other so formally."

The men hugged. Madeline smiled at the obvious affection between the two. But her smile faltered as she took in more details of the King's appearance, from the sunken cheeks to the deep blue network of veins beneath his skin. Saw the bittersweet regret on Eviana's face as the Princess watched her father. Realization hit.

The King wasn't just sick. He was dying.

Nicholai tried to keep his eyes on the easels, the folder in front of him, anything but her.

It proved almost impossible.

She'd opted for a cream-colored dress with, if he wasn't mistaken, an actual petticoat beneath that made the wide skirt flare out. The dress, he realized with a small smile, was covered in a pattern of vintage airplane blueprints. Her navy blazer and matching belt added the right touch of professionalism to an outfit that was purely Juliette. Creative, whimsical and unique.

Frustrated, he looked down at the brochure, but not before seeing Eviana's pondering gaze and hint of a teasing smile. He inwardly cursed. He hadn't gone into detail about what had happened

between him and Madeline in Paris, other than
to admit that he found Madeline intriguing. But
a sister as perceptive and nosy as Eviana hadn't
needed much to piece together that something significant had happened.

"We are ready."

Nausea settled in the pit of his stomach. Once
his father's voice had boomed out to the thousands
of people in Kelna, addressing crowds at festivals,
holiday celebrations and other royal events. Now
those tasks had fallen to Nicholai, along with numerous others, as his father's illness took its toll
on his lungs, his energy, everything that had made
Ivan great.

*A leader does not let personal matters take
them away from their duty to the people.*

His father's oft-spoken words centered him. He
raised his head and found Madeline watching him.
Sadness tinged her gaze as her eyes flickered to
Ivan, then down at her clasped hands. Her throat
moved as she swallowed hard.

She knows.

Instead of stirring concern or even anger, the
realization provided comfort. When she raised
her head again, she didn't look at him with pity or
concern or doubt. Her gaze radiated compassion
and an understanding rooted in the shared sense
of losing someone one loved.

Ivan slowly eased down into a chair. Nicholai
and Eviana followed suit. J.T., Andrew and Julie

all took chairs closer to the front of the table. Madeline and Chris stood in the center in front of the covered easels. Chris leaned down and said something to Madeline that brought a smile to her face.

Nicholai's chest tightened. Four weeks. Four weeks Madeline and Chris had been working together. Chris seemed far more interested in Madeline than she did him. A fact that brought little relief when he remembered that when this project was over, Madeline would return to Kansas City and live out the rest of her life thousands of miles away.

While he would stay here and serve as king.

"Please," Ivan said with a smile. "Begin."

Madeline nodded, tucking a stray lock of hair behind her ear. She breathed in deeply, glanced down and then looked back up. Calm softened her expression as she made eye contact with each person in the room.

Bravo, Madeline.

Proud of her, of seeing her in her element, Nicholai sat back and gave her his undivided attention.

Madeline dived into a summary of what she and her team had considered as they put together the designs for the initial proposal. She talked not just with her voice but with her hands, her facial expressions; the passion she'd felt for Kelna when she'd first glimpsed it from the air evident in her animated gestures, her excited tone.

She glossed over the history of the country,

rightly assuming the people present knew far more than she did. Although, Nicholai acknowledged, the facts she did cite rolled off her tongue like she'd been studying Kelna for years instead of weeks. She rattled off the architectural styles used throughout the palace.

"Which led us to your request." She turned and placed one hand on the first easel. "To bring the Grand Ballroom into the twenty-first century."

The room fell silent as Madeline lifted the cover off the first easel. The schematic drawing mirrored the first page in their folder. Circular in nature, the drawings noted walls made almost entirely of glass.

"The third and fourth pages in your folder are artistic renderings of what we imagined for the ballroom. Our design blends with the rest of the palace while bringing it into the twenty-first century," Madeline continued as she moved to the second easel. "It honors the past and everything that brought your country to this moment of change."

She lifted the cover. This drawing turned the flat two-dimensional design into a jaw-dropping reality. Marble steps swept up to the main entrance of the ballroom. Recessed lighting on the stairs made the limestone glow. At the top, two double doors set into a vaulted archway welcomed visitors. The walls were fashioned of glass and curved into a rounded shape, with marble pillars every dozen feet to hold up an elegant domed roof built of material in the same shade of red as the roofs of Lepa Plavi.

Conflicting emotions tightened Nicholai's chest. He liked the traditional elements, the use of the pillars and arches.

So much glass… Madeline's drawings were stunning, no doubt about it. Part of him understood the appeal. The current ballroom would be gutted, the new ballroom expanded out onto a green space with stunning views. The glass would give nearly a three-hundred-and-sixty-degree perspective on some of Kelna's most incredible scenery.

But it would also be a huge change. The most modern exterior update the palace had ever received.

Nicholai liked to think of himself as a forward-thinking man. One who had accepted the country's need to modernize.

It was also coming fast. Too fast.

The last cover came off, revealing the imagined interior. A grand chandelier hung from the top of the dome. More recessed lighting built into the simple but elegant white molding above the glass made the interior of the dome glow. The walls were finished in the palest of golds, a color that shone under both the light from above and the sunlight streaming in through the large windows.

"It's stunning."

Nicholai glanced at his sister. She was gazing at

the designs with a rapturous expression. Resentment crept over him, surprising and unwelcome but present nonetheless. Eviana fulfilled her role in multiple ways, including serving as the patron of numerous charities and sitting on committees for education, the new hospital and tourism.

But ever since they were children, their roles had been clear. Nicholai would one day inherit the throne and rule with a queen by his side. Eviana would support, but never lead. Kelna had had ruling queens before. The line of succession, however, had always favored the firstborn, with the primary responsibilities falling to the heir and their spouse.

It hadn't been something Nicholai had ever questioned. But as Kelna grew, Ivan stepped back from more of his royal duties, simply because he couldn't physically handle them anymore. Nicholai couldn't stop the occasional feeling of being stranded out in the middle of the ocean on a ship bravely charging through the waves, even as they rose higher and higher, lapping at the deck and threatening to pull it under at a moment's notice.

He blinked and looked away. It wasn't Eviana's fault. She was doing what she had been raised to do, as was he. She loved their father just as much and was taking his failing health hard. She had little memory of their mother, who had passed when Eviana was only two years old from an infection that had moved quickly and savagely.

Losing Ivan would be the first major loss she would remember. Begrudging her for the order of her birth and the easier load of duties she carried was selfish at best.

"Thank you," Madeline said with a deferential bow of her head in Eviana's direction. She motioned to the navy folders on the table in front of them, marked by Forge's logo. "Inside, you'll find everything you see here, which includes the layouts of the ballroom and how it will align with the existing palace."

"Normally the artistic designs are not included in the first presentation," J.T. added. "But we're fortunate to have someone with Madeline's twin talents of precision and creativity."

Madeline smiled slightly at her mentor. Something heavy settled in Nicholai's chest. Madeline wasn't just great at her job. She loved it. He'd asked himself more than once in their time apart if there was some way around their circumstances. A possibility for them to get to know each other.

But there was no point. He belonged in Kelna. Asking her to give up her career, her life back in America, would be like asking him to give up the crown.

"Thank you, Miss Delvine." Ivan nodded to the folder open before him. "A moment for my children and me to review, please."

"Of course."

Silence fell, permeated only by the whisper of

paper as the royals flipped through the carefully prepared materials. The team at Forge had been thorough. Nicholai knew he had pushed them on the deadline. But the palace was paying for the expedited process. If it meant Ivan would see the finished ballroom, hopefully for celebrating a royal wedding, then it was worth every penny.

But unless his father, who favored the tradition and history of the palace, agreed with Eviana, they would be asking for Forge to revise their proposal and opt for something more in line with the rest of the palace's aesthetic.

Ivan sat back and steepled his fingers in front of him as he regarded Madeline with a thoughtful gaze.

"I agree with my daughter."

Nicholai's head snapped around.

"Thank you, Your Highness… Majesty."

Pink tinged Madeline's cheeks at her faux pas. Ivan waved it away with a quick flick of his hand.

"Do not trouble yourself over titles here, Miss Delvine. The designs are wonderful."

All heads turned to Nicholai.

"It is very well done."

Madeline's expression tightened for a brief moment before she forced a slight smile to her face.

"But you have concerns?"

He hesitated. He didn't want to hurt her. But, he reminded himself, she was a professional. She deserved the truth.

"The modernity. It wasn't what I pictured."

"What would you change?"

He drummed his fingers on the tabletop, not wanting to share the tangled web of emotions behind his reticence.

"I don't know." He shot her a smile. "If my father and sister approve, any minor concerns of mine don't mean anything."

Madeline frowned. "But they do. This is your home. If something needs to be changed—"

"Nothing needs to be changed." Suddenly frustrated with himself for his irrational feelings about a damned building, and about Madeline's pressing for his opinion, he responded to her tight smile with one of his own. "It has my seal of approval. *Otac?*"

Ivan nodded, his eyes cautious as he glanced between Nicholai and Madeline.

"Good. Eviana?"

Self-contempt dug deep into his skin, little barbs that pricked his pride and his sense of honor, as the excited light in his sister's eyes dimmed, replaced by concern.

"I do like it. But I agree with Madeline. If you—"

"Then it's settled." Nicholai nodded to Madeline, Chris and the rest of the team. "If you could put everything into a report for the Citizens' Committee, we'll forward it to them for review."

He was about to make his exit when Ivan stopped him with a raised hand.

"The ball."

His jaw tightened. "Of course. Would you like to extend the formal invitation, Eviana? It was your idea."

"Yes." Eviana recovered enough to smile at the team. "We're hosting a ball this Saturday. It's a national holiday and we've invited a number of public service employees, palace staff and some international guests. The Citizens' Committee meets the Friday before and will have an answer before the ball. If they're approved, we'd love to unveil the designs and have you there as our guests."

"And even if they aren't approved, we would still be honored to have you," Ivan added with a comforting smile.

Nicholai looked away. His father had always excelled at building relationships, at making people feel seen and heard. From what little he could remember of his mother, she had been the same. He enjoyed talking with people, yes, and knew he was an adequate speaker. Some had even compared him to his father, words he had taken as a compliment for years but now sounded ghoulish in the light of his father's illness. Unfortunately, engaging with the public often fell by the wayside as he focused his time and attention onto his ever-growing to-do list.

"I've never been to a royal ball." J.T. grinned. "Ivan, I hope you have a suit I can borrow."

"Eviana is familiar with several shops in Lepa

Plavi that would be happy to supply you with evening wear." Nicholai glanced at his sister, who nodded. "And of course, you're welcome to stay at the palace."

The others quickly agreed. Madeline was the last to respond, and then only with a tiny smile and a soft "thank you." Their eyes met for one heart-pounding second. And then she looked away as she began to collect the designs.

He contemplated staying, waiting for a moment to talk to her and explain why he had hesitated. To reassure her that it was nothing to do with her work and everything to do with the inner turmoil he fought as he faced inheriting his father's throne.

He stood, hesitated. Then, with a nod and quick quirk of his lips that passed for a smile, walked out the door. Sharing with her would mean acknowledging the pull he felt toward her, the desire to be in her company. Feelings he had no business pursuing when his future was tied to his country and his crown.

CHAPTER SIX

MADELINE SMOOTHED THE skirts of her dress as she hesitated next to a potted plant. The murmur of hundreds of voices rose and fell in the ballroom, backlit by the strains of a professional orchestra. People moved about, talking and sipping champagne, completely at ease in the gaudy surroundings. Even the garish colors and over-the-top paintings had been softened by the glow of candlelight.

The ball had kicked off half an hour ago. Madeline had spent far too much time debating whether the off-the-shoulder scarlet gown she'd picked out from the nearly half dozen dresses Eviana had sent to her room was suitable. She'd barely made it down in time to hear King Ivan welcome his guests. The whispers that had circled around the ballroom like wildfire had been hard to ignore.

"He's so thin."

"Oh, no. I knew he was ill, but it's worse than I thought."

"Nicholai will be King before the year is out. I'm sure of it."

Her heart had broken for Nicholai, who had taken the stage shortly after his father. She'd seen men in tuxedos before. Alex had worn one to a black-tie gala at the National World War I Museum in Kansas City. But where Alex had tugged at his bow tie all evening and grumbled under his breath, Nicholai wore his with confidence. Coupled with his engaging smile and warm tone, it wasn't hard to picture him taking over the reins from his father and leading the country.

When he had officially announced the beginning of the ball, the room had erupted into applause.

Madeline's smile had disappeared as more than one elegantly clad woman had approached Nicholai. Some had murmured a quick word and shaken his hand or dipped into a curtsy. But several lingered, one being bold enough to lay her hand on his arm in a gesture of intimacy that made Madeline feel sick to her stomach.

"Are you hiding?"

Madeline started as Julie appeared beside her.

"More observing. I've never been to something like this."

"Me either." Julie grinned. "I'm starting with the food. My house is almost strictly pizza, macaroni and cheese, and grilled cheese sandwiches."

Madeline followed her to the buffet at the back, the tables draped in snow-white tablecloths and laden with food. Delicacies like marinated scampi, truffles and *fritule*, battered doughnut balls dusted with lemon zest and infused with rum, were artfully arranged on silver platters next to a glass tower, each layer covered in chocolates and bites of cheesecake drizzled in raspberry sauce. By the time Julie and Madeline had made it back to their table, their plates were loaded with nearly one of everything. Chris and Andrew had joined them. The camaraderie distracted Madeline enough for her to enjoy her food.

Nicholai walked onto the dance floor to formally open the ball with Eviana at his side. Whispered speculations flying around the room about the King not dancing with Eviana died as the two siblings laughed and smiled through the waltz.

Madeline smiled. She liked how close the royals were. The King exuded a quiet sense of power and a touch of reserve that was almost imperceptible. But she had yet to see him without kindness in his eyes or friendliness in his smile.

Eviana carried the same reserve as her father. Glimpses of a bubblier, sweet woman had come through. But those moments were fleeting, like she wasn't quite sure who to fully trust with seeing the true depth of her character.

And then there was Nicholai. A man who had yet to falter in public, but who struggled in private with the massive changes taking place in the Kingdom. A man who loved his father and, she suspected, worked hard to keep his grief private as he prepared to lead.

She'd been disappointed at his response to the designs. Yet she'd sensed something else lurking beneath the surface, a suspicion confirmed by his strong reaction to her prompting him.

It had hurt to see him walk away. But she'd reminded herself, in the long run it didn't matter. The designs had been approved, both by the royal family and by the Citizens' Committee. Part of the King's welcome had included the announcement of the new ballroom and directing guests to view the mock-ups on prominent display by the main door.

A night of triumph. She needed to buck up and enjoy the moment instead of ruminating over someone else's opinion.

The music wound down. Nicholai and Eviana separated. Nicholai bowed as his sister dropped into a graceful curtsy. Thunderous applause broke out as the crowd stood. Nicholai accepted a microphone from a palace aide.

"Let the celebrations begin!"

People moved onto the dance floor. An older man with a thick gray beard and a stunning blonde approached Nicholai. Clad in a black gown that followed her tall, slender figure, the woman curtsied as if she'd been doing so her whole life. The bearded man said something and Nicholai smiled down at the woman.

Madeline's heart twisted. Frustrated with herself, she pushed back her chair.

"Maddie?" Chris shot her a smile. "Want to dance?"

She wavered. As she'd watched Nicholai and Eviana move through the dance with graceful movements, she'd imagined what it would be like to dance like that. Not just dance, but dance at an actual royal ball wearing an incredible gown gifted to her by a real-life princess.

"Go on." Andrew nudged her. "I'll dance with Julie if you dance with Chris."

"Now you have to!" Julie said as she hopped up. "Don't leave me hanging."

Madeline laughed. "Peer pressure wins again."

Chris took her hand and led her to the dance floor, Julie and Andrew trailing behind them. Out of the corner of her eye, Madeline saw Nicholai take the blonde in his arms and begin to dance. Her stomach knotted. She turned away and focused on the man in front of her. The one who hadn't told her there could never be anything between him. The one she wished she could feel something for besides friendship.

Chris settled a hand at her waist and smiled down at her. "Ready?"

"To trip over my own feet? Yes."

He tugged her a fraction closer. She didn't resist. He surprised her by confidently guiding her into a turn before pulling her back to his chest. She let out a surprised laugh.

"Where did you learn to dance?"

"I took a ballroom dancing class in college."

"Ballroom dancing? In college?"

"Also took scuba diving, an introduction to painting and beginner's French."

"An eclectic mix."

"And a great way to meet women."

She laughed again. The easy conversation, coupled with dancing with someone who knew what they were doing, the light glowing from the chandeliers above, all of it swept away her earlier agitation. Determined to enjoy herself, she agreed to another dance with Chris, followed by a dance with Andrew and even one with J.T.

When she glanced at the towering grandfather clock behind the buffet, she realized over an hour had passed.

"I need champagne," Julie said with a laugh as she joined Madeline back at their table.

"I need water."

"Yes." Julie glanced over her shoulder. "I saw you and Chris dancing together."

"He's a good dancer."

"Any potential there?"

Madeline shrugged. "Chris is a good friend. But I'm not looking to date anyone right now."

Julie's face sobered. "Sorry. I shouldn't have pried."

"It's okay. I think Chris would like for there to be more, but after Alex, I just need time by myself."

"Wise." Julie plucked two champagne glasses off a passing tray. "I'm someone who didn't find her Prince Charming until the second wedding because I rushed into my first marriage after a bad breakup. Having some time to yourself is very smart."

"Thank you."

Madeline clinked her glass against Julie's and took a small sip.

"I think I could use some fresh air."

"Another smart idea." Julie glanced back at the ballroom. "I'm going to take advantage of not having to wake up with my kids in the morning and dance a little more."

"Go on. I'll join you in a bit."

Madeline drifted along the edges of the ballroom, her eyes roaming over the glamorously dressed people, the synchronized movements of the orchestra as she listened to the rise and fall of conversation in over a dozen languages. It was as close to perfect as a moment could get. Her nerves tangled with excitement and satisfaction. She was in a brand-new country with coworkers who felt more like family, and the biggest project she had worked on to date had been accepted by a literal king, prince and princess.

Life was good.

As she neared the glass doors leading out into

the garden, she glanced over her shoulder and nearly stumbled over the hem of her dress. Nicholai was back on the dance floor, this time with one arm wrapped intimately around the waist of a voluptuous brunette he appeared to know very well. He was smiling down at her as she spoke, his attention focused solely on the woman in his arms. One hand came up and rested on his lapel as she leaned up and whispered something in his ear that made him throw back his head and laugh.

The sudden, crushing disappointment floored her. Yes, she was attracted to Nicholai, had thoroughly enjoyed their kiss in Paris. Getting to know him a little bit on a personal level, to learn more about the man behind the crown, had made her like him even more.

But she had written off her interest as something that would pass with time. Never had she entertained the possibility that seeing him with someone else would matter. Let alone two someones. He hadn't struck her as a playboy.

Yeah, because you're so good at judging men.

For the first time in her life, she felt a crack in her heart, one that hinted her feelings went far deeper. She'd never experienced anything like this with Alex. The strength of her emotions, coupled with how rapidly they'd developed, frightened her.

Nicholai and his partner spun. His head came up. His gaze locked on Madeline's. She inhaled sharply, then picked up her skirt and hurried out the door. There were a few people milling about the terrace and a young couple walking up the short flight of stairs from the garden. Lanterns flickered along the stone balustrade. A full moon glowed bright over the palace and dusted the waves of the Adriatic with a sheen of silver.

"Champagne?"

Madeline nodded to the waiter and accepted a flute off the tray. Having something to hold in her hands steadied her. She moved down the stairs, taking a sip as she crossed the grass toward the rose garden. Music drifted out from the open doors of the ballroom, but the farther she walked, the more it served as a background, the lyrical strains adding a touch of magic to her surroundings.

She walked beneath an arch of white roses that glowed in the moonlight, breathing in the deep, heady scent of rose petals and a faintly sweet smell coming from plants dripping with lavender blooms shaped like little bells. The garden, she realized with a small degree of delight, was comprised of a series of circles. The circles themselves were cobblestone paths. In between the circles were carefully tended beds of roses. The entire garden was contained by a series of stone arches that matched the stonework she had seen in Lepa Plavi. At the center of the garden stood a magnificent, tiered fountain.

She moved from circle to circle, stopping here

and there to inhale the various fragrances. When she finally made her way to the center, she stopped, staring at the play of water as it fell.

A flash of white beyond the fountain caught her eye. Curious, she circled the water feature and found another path, one fashioned of pale stone that wound and twisted through a thick grove of evergreen trees.

Then she emerged from the trees into the closest thing to Heaven she'd ever seen.

A white terrace had been built on a cliff overlooking the sea, the intricate stonework surrounded by a balustrade with thick columns that reminded her of ancient Rome. The moon made the terrace shine as if it were lit from within.

She moved to the edge, let one hand rest on the cool stone as she watched the waves rise and fall a hundred feet below. A sigh escaped her lips as her thoughts turned back to the Prince dancing in the ballroom with a woman who looked very at ease in his arms. She would have to deal with whatever emotions Nicholai had stirred in her, and soon, so that it didn't affect her work. She'd been fortunate that it hadn't been a problem so far.

She also needed to do it for her own sake. As much as she loved her stories of romance, there was no such thing as love at first sight. And even if there were, she had no interest in falling for a man who lived half a world away.

The footsteps behind her had her whirling about.

Champagne sloshed over the rim of her glass and spilled onto her hand.

Nicholai stood just a few feet behind her, his hands held up in a gesture of surrender.

"You have got to stop sneaking up on me," she gasped.

"Well, if you would stop sneaking out to odd places, maybe I wouldn't have to follow you."

She narrowed her eyes at him. "Seriously?"

He grimaced. "Bad joke."

"Very."

They stared at each other for a long moment. A sudden urge to laugh crept up Madeline's throat. She tried to hold it back, but ended up letting out a very unladylike snort before she gave in and laughed.

Nicholai arched a brow even as one corner of his mouth twitched.

"What?"

"I almost bashed you over the head with a champagne glass. First a wine bottle, and then a champagne flute."

"If I didn't know any better, I would think you a very poor assassin. Or at least an attempted one."

Madeline contemplated the remaining bit of champagne in her glass. "If it makes you feel any better, I'd rather not waste it on your head."

"Comforting," he replied dryly.

She held up the glass in a toast to him. Suddenly shy, she took another sip to give herself something else to focus on.

"What is this place?"

Nicholai glanced around. "I'd actually forgotten about it. I think my great-great-grandmother had this commissioned in the late nineteenth century."

"It's beautiful."

"It is."

She leaned against the banister. "Do you come out here often?"

"Do you mean why did I follow you out here?" At her nod, he approached to stand next to her at the banister. "I saw you come out. You looked upset when you left the ballroom."

Embarrassed, she looked back over the sea. "Just a little overwhelmed, I think. There's a lot going on."

She felt him move closer. Her breathing grew heavy as she felt his presence at her back.

"Did Chris upset you?"

Startled, she looked at him. "No. Why would you ask that?"

The thunderous expression on his face took her by surprise.

"I saw how much the two of you were dancing together. Didn't know if you had had a lovers' spat."

"Chris and I are not, and never will be, lovers."

"Does he know that?"

Guilt surfaced and dug its claws deep into her skin. "I haven't explicitly said no. I need to."

"Yes, you do. Because I see the way he looks at you."

"Oh, really? Is it the same way the curvy brunette you were just dancing with looks at you?"

Nicholai's brows drew together. "Amara?"

"Sure. The gorgeous woman you were dancing with, who could be a brunette version of Marilyn Monroe."

"You noticed."

"How could one not notice? She's beautiful and sexy and—"

"Would you like me to introduce you?"

Madeline contemplated if sticking out her tongue would be too childish.

"Amara is a friend."

"Nicholai," she said softly, "you don't have to explain anything to me. I know we didn't get a chance to have a full discussion about what happened between us in Paris, but it was one hour. One kiss. After this project is over, I go back to Kansas City, and you stay here to be an actual king." She smiled at him in what she hoped was a reassuring manner that didn't reveal the ache growing inside her at the thought of never seeing him again. "You don't owe me anything."

"Well spoken, Miss Delvine."

Put out by his casual acceptance, she inclined her head to him.

"Thank you. Now, I think I'll rejoin—"

"Except there's one problem." Nicholai stepped in front of her. "I haven't been able to stop thinking of you since Paris."

Madeline nearly dropped her glass. "What?"

"I know that nothing can happen between us, nothing permanent. I have my life here—you have your life back in America." His hand came up, hesitated in the air between them, then settled on her face with such tenderness it made her eyes grow hot. "I think about that hour I spent with you on the rooftop in Paris. It was the first time in a very long time that I was able to be…" His voice trailed off.

"Just Nick," she prompted softly.

"Just Nick," he echoed. "To forget about the responsibilities, the committees, the economic forums, all the change happening in my life. And when I saw you dancing with Chris, I wanted to cross the ballroom and rip him away from you. I'm not a violent man, Madeline. But seeing him touch you…" His voice trailed off as he stared deep into her eyes. "I could barely stand it."

Madeline's breath froze in her chest. One wrong step and she would fall, fall further than she ever had with Alex.

And yet, whispered a tempting little voice, *what if you fly?*

Slowly, she set down her champagne glass, then held out her hand.

"May I have this dance?"

Nicholai's mouth curved into a reluctant smile. "I'm supposed to ask you."

"So ask."

He captured her hand in his, brought it up to his lips and grazed a kiss over her knuckles. She swallowed hard.

"Miss Delvine, would you do me the honor of sharing a dance with me?"

"I'd love to." The faintest notes of music drifted across the lawn, over the roses and through the trees to the cliff. Chris had been a fun dance partner, but Nicholai was a master, sweeping her into elegant turns as he kept one hand firmly at her waist and the other wrapped around her fingers, leading her in a dance she had only seen in movies. Had she thought earlier in the ballroom that life had been perfect? Because it paled in comparison to this moment.

Nicholai held her close, the intimacy of his hand at her waist thrilling her senses and making her feel like the most beautiful woman in the world.

Too soon, the music wound down. They drifted to a stop next to the banister, the distant roar of the waves crashing on the beach below eclipsing the dwindling music. She wanted to keep going, to pretend that real life was not waiting on the other side of the evergreens.

And knew that to pretend anything different would only be delaying the inevitable.

She stepped back, dipped into a curtsy.

"Thank you. Your Highness."

Nicholai's face tightened.

"You know as well as I do," she said quietly

even as her heart twisted in her chest, "this can't go anywhere."

Nicholai hesitated, his lips parting as if to say something in protest, before they thinned back into a line.

Her heart felt like it was breaking, but if she could spare him some of the pain she was experiencing, she wanted to. She'd seen the hurt in his eyes when he looked at his father, the uncertainty as he gazed out over an evolving Kingdom from the window of a plane. His life was here. Hers was not.

She started to walk around him, to rejoin the ball. Nicholai's hand shot out, wrapped around her arm, and before she could say a word, he pulled her against him and claimed her lips with his own.

She kissed him back, throwing her arms around his neck and pouring every emotion she had been fighting for the past month into their kiss.

He pulled her close, his mouth moving over hers with passion and a hint of desperation, as if he knew this would be the final time.

He pulled back. She didn't stop him, letting her arms fall to her sides. Slowly, she raised her eyes to his.

"It's a shame, isn't it?" she finally said.

When he didn't respond, she turned and walked away, the crack in her heart deepening with every step.

CHAPTER SEVEN

Nicholai awoke to a frantic pounding on his door. Groaning, he rolled over and glanced at the clock. It wasn't even 7:00 a.m. He pulled a pillow over his face, hoping whoever had dared to intrude this early after a ball that had kept him up past midnight would just go away.

The knocking intensified.

Exhausted and irritated, Nicholai flung back the covers and got out of bed. He pulled on his robe with swift movements before he stalked to the door.

"What—?"

"Oh, no." Eviana barreled into his room and slammed the door shut behind her. "I'm the only one who gets to ask questions this morning." She held up a newspaper. "The first of which is, what were you thinking?"

Frowning, he grabbed the newspaper. Dread crept over him and squeezed his chest with an iron grip as he realized what he was looking at.

The pictures splashed across the front page of the Kelnian national newspaper were almost as bad as the headline: "Is Kelna's Future King a Playboy?"

One picture featured him and the tall, blonde British Duchess Dario had introduced him to for the second dance. Another had caught him and Amara in the middle of a waltz. The photographer had managed to capture the perfect angle that showed off the sweetheart neckline of Amara's bodice and her rounded curves. The third...

Nicholai's fingers tightened on the paper. The third picture was of him and Madeline kissing on the cliffside terrace. Despite the graininess of the picture, it was clearly him.

The article featured detailed biographies of the duchess, Amara and Madeline. The duchess's biography included a summary of her wealth and lauded family background. Then it jumped into speculations on his and Amara's decade of friendship and rumors from supposed sources that there had always been "something more" between them.

But the one that made his blood boil were the gleeful sentences dedicated to Madeline's first trip to Kelna the month before. The reporter had gone so far as to rehash her childhood in Kansas City and include a mention about an ex-fiancé named Alex, a prominent lawyer back in Missouri.

The last paragraph about her broken engagement made his stomach twist. She'd said nothing about being engaged before.

But then again, when had they had time to discuss much of anything? Really, what did he know about her?

His eyes strayed back to the photo of him and Madeline locked in a passionate embrace. She stirred feelings he'd never experienced before. Not just attraction and warmth, but jealousy. The burning in his chest when he'd seen her dancing with Chris, the bitterness that had swept through him when she'd laughed up at the other man had bothered him. Was this infatuation? Obsession?

And now...now he was faced with the consequences of not being able to keep himself under control. Of letting his emotions over his father's illness, the numerous changes taking place in Kelna and his own doubts about taking the throne sway him from duty.

The desire to crumple the paper into a ball and hurl it in the trash nearly overcame his resolve. He set the paper down on his bed and moved to the window.

"Well?"

"Well, what?"

Eviana appeared next to him. "What are you going to do?"

"Talk with Father first. Then public affairs. Find out the best way to handle this."

"What about Madeline? Don't you think you should talk to her, too?"

"Eventually yes. But this is a palace affair."

Even as he said it, discomfort moved through

his chest. If she wasn't already, Madeline would become the focus of intense scrutiny in the coming days. She had made her desire to steer clear of any royal entanglements clear. She had a life, a career, family back home. Any woman he dated now would automatically be seen as a potential contender for the title of queen. The reminder soured his mood, fanned the flames of a growing anger. He had dated in his twenties, yes. A couple of casual relationships, and one lengthier relationship with an Italian countess that he thought might lead to the altar. But they had all ended, most due to the capriciousness of youth, a couple when one or both of them had realized that they were simply not right for each other.

But now he felt the pressure to be seen as dependable, stable. That meant a prince with a princess by his side, one who would help lead the country. At one point he had thought he'd had all the time in the world to find a woman, fall in love and propose because it was something they both wanted. Yet as the media scrutiny grew, the women he was introduced to seemed more focused on his crown than on him.

Although, he thought as a dull throbbing started to pulse in his temples, he was no better. Letting Dario put together a list of suitable candidates and reviewing their backgrounds as if he were interviewing someone for a job instead of spending the rest of their life with him.

Which made his situation with Madeline all the more painful. That night in Paris, when she had not known who he was, had been one of the best nights of his life in recent memory. Her being a dynamic, intelligent woman with a happy personality that invited one to enjoy life as much as she did made his future look all the more bleak by comparison.

"It will affect her, too."

Nicholai narrowed his eyes at his sister.

"Did I miss you and Madeline becoming best friends? You just met her."

"I like her." She planted her hands on her hips in a gesture that reminded him of when she had been four and thrown a royal tantrum in the reception room after their father had announced that he would be gone for two weeks at a summit in Spain. "Even if I didn't, it's the right thing to do. Especially with how you feel about each other."

"You don't know what you're talking about."

Instead of backing down from the icy censure in his voice, Eviana drew herself up to her full height. Even being nearly a foot shorter than he was, she still made an impressive figure as she poked him square in the chest.

"I know what I saw, Nicholai. However you two decide to handle it is up to you. If you both want to pretend like there's nothing going on, even though anyone with eyes can see that you two obviously care about each other, then that's your affair." She picked up the newspaper, dangled it from her fingers with a smirk. "Or rather anyone with a subscription to the *Kelna National News*."

Nicholai picked up a pillow from the nearby sofa and launched it at his sister's head. She ducked and scampered for the door.

"Talk to Madeline first."

"You don't know what you're talking about, Eviana. You don't have to worry about things like this."

"Only because you won't let me help."

Confused, he stared at her. "What are you talking about?"

"Nothing." She shook her head. "Wrong time, wrong place. Please, consider talking to her first."

"I can't, Eviana. The situation has to be contained."

"Does 'contained' mean she won't be able to work on the ballroom?"

He scrubbed a hand over his face. *Probably.* It wouldn't be appropriate to have the woman he'd been caught kissing working on the ballroom while he searched for a wife.

"Most likely not. It wouldn't be in the best interests of the palace or the country."

"Spoken like a politician." The disappointed expression on his sister's face cut him deep. "Looks like you're ready to be king after all."

With that parting shot, she moved out of the room. The door shut behind her with a click, the sound echoing in Nicholai's head as he turned back to stare out over the sea.

The need for his father's guidance tugged at him, urged him to seek out the King and talk with him.

But the man who had been thrust to the edge of inheriting the Kingdom, who would have to make decisions on his own far sooner than he had expected, resisted. He was a grown man. A man who would lead over half a million people and have to make split-second decisions that affected their lives and the lives of future generations. A notion his own father had impressed upon him from the time he'd been a teenager.

"We won't always make the right decisions, son. But we have to make the best ones we know in the moment, not just for this generation, but for future generations to come."

Nicholai scrubbed a hand over his face, then wrapped his fingers around his jaw. One of his first major crises, and it all came down to not being able to keep his hands off a feisty American architect.

A knock sounded on his door.

"Go away, Eviana."

The door creaked open. Nicholai spun around. "I said…"

His voice trailed off. Madeline stood in the door, wearing a white robe over a T-shirt and pajama shorts. Her hair hung in blond, tussled waves about her face. The lack of makeup enhanced her youth, drove his sense of guilt even deeper.

"Madeline."

She closed the door behind her.

"We need to talk."

Madeline's heart sank as Nicholai stared at her with an unreadable expression on his face. He watched her for a moment before he turned away and began to pace.

She'd woken up to a barrage of text messages and missed phone calls. Screenshots of her kiss with Nicholai were now flashed across the worldwide media. Embarrassment had ruled as she'd flipped through everything from congratulations to a mortifying message from her mother asking what she had gotten into.

But as her initial panic had subsided, her mind had turned to Nicholai. The drama she faced right now wouldn't impact her future much. Yes, she didn't relish her name popping up in articles years from now if she ever decided to work for another firm.

But despite the mention of her broken engagement, the writer had painted her in a neutral light, focusing primarily on her career and how she had come to be at the ball in Kelna. It was Nicholai who had been vilified with a list of women he'd been spotted with in the past year as well as a rather flowery description of his dance with Amara. He'd been painted the aggressor, a playboy indulging in his position.

"I don't have the time to discuss this right now, Madeline."

Frustration surged through her. "Then when is the right time to discuss this?"

"Later."

"No." She moved closer. "This affects both of us."

"I'm aware."

She reached out, grabbed onto the back of a chair with both hands and squeezed tight. "What can I do?"

Nicholai pinched the bridge of his nose, and let out a harsh breath. "The best thing you could possibly do right now is go back to your room and stay there until I've talked with the public relations department."

"Hide?"

He whirled then, tension vibrating from his frame. "Yes, hide. This is my world, not yours. You don't know what could happen in the next hour, two hours, twenty-four hours. My leadership has already been called into question by that blasted article. The people who have invested in Kelna's advancement will, at the very least, have questions. The kind of questions that carry underlying threats, such as if the stability of Kelna is not guaranteed, neither is their money."

The full weight of how a simple kiss could affect hundreds of thousands of people hit Madeline with the force of a freight train.

"Nicholai... I'm sorry."

"Don't apologize. It only makes it worse. I saw you go out. I followed you. I put you in this position. I put the country in this position." He stopped pacing and turned, his face thunderous. "Go back to your room, Madeline. Someone from Public Affairs will be by soon." He sighed. "I'll have to speak to your team at some point today, too."

Alarm skittered through her. "My team? Why?"

"I don't like contemplating this, but..." His voice trailed off as he closed his eyes. When he opened them, he looked at her with a regret that turned her alarm into full-on panic. "I don't think Forge Architecture continuing to work on the ballroom will be a good fit. Not with this press."

Shock rendered her speechless as shame kept her feet glued to the floor. The biggest job J.T. had ever landed. She'd put that all at risk. Yes, Nicholai had followed her, initiated their kiss. But she'd asked him to dance. She'd kissed him back. She'd been a more than willing participant to it all.

Her mind scrambled, trying to grasp onto something, anything she could do.

"There has to be something that can make this better."

"If you can somehow convince the world I'm not a playboy who toys with women's emotions, then yes, by all means, do something."

"What would reassure the investors? Anyone who might doubt your ability to lead?"

"Nothing." Nicholai closed his eyes, breathed in and then out before opening them again, his brown eyes dark with pain. "Nothing except being engaged or married. A clear sign that I am not, in fact, a playboy."

The mad idea entered her head. She batted it away. No. It was too ridiculous.

But it was a stubborn idea, one that slipped in and coaxed her, inch by inch, to say it out loud.

"What if I pretended to be your fiancée?"

CHAPTER EIGHT

WHAT?

Nicholai stared at Madeline. Surely, he had heard her wrong.

"Excuse me?"

She looked as though she'd swallowed something sour, her lips pinching together as pink bloomed in her cheeks. But then she squared her shoulders and raised her chin.

"What if we pretended to be engaged?"

"This isn't a romance novel, Madeline. This is real life with real people's livelihoods and an entire country at stake."

Her eyes narrowed. He stifled a groan. He'd hurt her.

"You said your leadership had been called into question. That the people funding all the development going on might pull out. My problem is on a smaller scale, but my employer and coworkers could lose the largest project they've ever worked on. Wouldn't revealing a secret engagement be less—" her blush deepened as she cleared her throat "—scandalous? Reassure your investors and the rest of the country. And Forge could stay on the project."

The more she talked, the less crazy it sounded. Logical, even.

He would still have to deal with the press coverage surrounding Amara. She was a beautiful woman, but he had never entertained romantic thoughts of her, had barely even seen her over the past two years as she'd pursued her career in England. A quick conversation and statements from both the palace and her representatives would smooth that over. And the Duchess had been mere conjecture. Emphasizing that the prime minister had introduced the two of them would squelch any rumors.

But Madeline... The picture was damning, to say the least. The photographer had caught them at just the right moment, wrapped in each other's arms, her hand on his face.

Yes, that one would be much more difficult to explain away. Never mind, he thought crossly, that he was a man and should have a moment or two out of the spotlight. A moment to kiss a woman he found interesting and engaging and kind, but had no future with.

It seemed life would prefer he not even have those precious seconds of normality.

He looked back at Madeline. She looked so young, so innocent, standing there with rumpled hair and a worried wrinkle between her brows. She had made it clear that her home was in Kansas City, that her career was important to her.

There was no future for them. And he couldn't bring himself to enter into an engagement, even a fake one, knowing that it would end.

"I appreciate your offer, Madeline. It's very generous. But there has to be a better way."

A blankness swept across her face, erasing all hint of emotion.

"Of course." She dipped her head. "I'll be in my room if you need me."

And then she was gone.

With a groan, he sank down onto the edge of his bed.

"...there has to be a better way."

He certainly could have phrased that differently.

Another knock sounded on his door.

"Come in," he called wearily.

The door swung open and King Ivan walked in. Nicholai rushed forward.

"*Otac*, what are you doing up?"

"I'm sick, *sin*, not dead."

Ivan's fingers clutched the knobby head of his cane as he moved into the room and chose a chair close to the door. He sank into it, his breathing labored.

Nicholai's hands tightened into fists at his sides. He wanted to turn away, knew without a doubt that his actions last night and the resulting media frenzy this morning had heaped stress on his father's already overburdened shoulders.

But he stood his ground, prepared to face whatever punishment his father thought best.

"How are you this morning?" Ivan asked in a raspy voice as he settled in amongst the cushions.

One eyebrow shot up. "If I said 'well,' would you believe me?"

Ivan chuckled. "Not in the slightest." His face sobered, his pale eyes far kinder than they should have been, given the circumstances. "*Sin*, you made a mistake."

"I did." Nicholai sat down in a chair across from his father and threaded his fingers together. "I have no excuse. I let my emotions and attraction to Madeline get the better of me."

"Nicholai. You are allowed to a kiss a beautiful woman. I was referring more to kissing her in a public place."

He stalked around the room. "But I shouldn't have kissed her at all. Not when I'm supposed to be married…soon."

Ivan's face tightened. Despite the illness that ravaged his body, he still maintained the regality that had set the tone of his reign. A man who loved his people and his country, but also knew when to invoke a stricter, at times harsher, leadership. He did not suffer fools or those who preyed on them.

"Our public relations department tells me the photo was taken with a long-range lens. It was outside the palace grounds and a clear violation of our privacy. Had it not been you, it could have very well been one of our other guests."

"Except it wasn't another guest. It was me. And now my ability to lead has been called into question."

Anger flared, made his muscles tremble with the sudden fierceness of it. His latest struggles with taking over the throne, of replacing his father, suddenly seemed foolish when confronted with the possibility of having to step aside, to forgo the crown that had been in his family for generations. While he didn't think it would require a drastic act like abdicating, he would do it if it meant keeping the patronage of the wealthy organizations pouring money and resources into Kelna.

Ivan sighed. "Things were much simpler when I took the crown. There were photographers, yes, but not like this. You will replace the Forge team?"

Nicholai stood and began to pace. "Most likely, yes. I'll never be able to get rid of the speculation with her nearby."

Ivan nodded, even though his expression was sad. Guilt dug deeper into Nicholai's skin, sharp little barbs he wasn't sure he'd ever be able to rid himself of. The results of his actions grew worse by the minute.

"And Madeline is not a consideration?"

"No. She would not give up her life in America."

"Work can be done from almost anywhere these days."

"True. But Parliament still has to approve my choice of bride. They prefer nobility and prestige over personal preference."

Based on his last conversation with Dario, he was certain of it. Besides, what was the point in pressing the issue anyway? Of creating more stress and change when it wouldn't change Madeline's mind.

"But you don't know if you don't ask—"

"She's made it clear her heart is in Missouri."

Ivan blinked at Nicholai's curt tone. Inwardly cursing, Nicholai held his father's gaze even though he wanted nothing more than to look away.

"This is best for everyone. I promise you," he added at the doubtful expression on his father's face, "I'm doing the right thing."

Ivan sighed, the sound hoarse and raspy. "I trust you, *moj sin*. I simply wish you would extend others the same trust. Not try to conquer everything on your own."

Nicholai frowned. His father's words echoed Eviana's sentiments before she'd walked out. It bothered him that his family thought he didn't trust them.

Before he could reply, Ivan spoke again.

"Your and Madeline's pictures have already reached the United States. They're jumping on the story. Public Affairs has arranged for a press conference at eleven this morning so you can address the nation."

Nicholai nodded. "Done."

"Normally I would advise against a conference and let Public Affairs release a statement. But I've already had calls from Verde Construction and two of the shipping firms in Greece." Ivan's voice firmed, his irritation evident. "They're asking for reassurances that last night was simply bad press and not a pattern."

The knife twisted deeper. *"Otac—"*

"No. I disagree with how they're handling this media attention. You, and our country, have shown them how capable we are over the last year. But we are beholden to them for many things that will impact Kelna. I don't require an explanation, *moj sin.* Just a promise to fix this, to show them you can handle things."

Handle things.

A euphemism for what so many seemed to know, yet no one would talk about. Unless a miracle happened, his father would be dead within a year. He had wanted to lead, yes, to follow his father's and grandfather's legacy. But not like this. Not with his assuming the role because he took the crown from his father's grave.

Ivan started to rise.

"Let me—"

"Please." Ivan held up a wrinkled hand. "Let

me do the small things. Better to struggle than not be able to do them at all."

He finally got to his feet and walked toward the door, the thud of his cane on the floor echoing throughout the room. He turned and gave his son a small smile. "You will be king one day soon, *sin*. I trust you to make the right decision for our people. While we serve them first, I hope you will also consider yourself in this equation, too."

The click of the door closing sounded like a gate slamming shut on a prison cell.

Nicholai turned and moved to his windows with slow, deliberate movements. Inside him, anger and fear raged. Anger at himself, at the blasted photographer, at the heavens for cursing a good man and a good leader with such a terrible illness.

And fear. Fear that he would make the wrong choice. He'd already made one last night—he'd told himself repeatedly as he'd followed Madeline into the gardens that he should let her go.

But he hadn't. Seeing her laugh and dance without him had made him crave her presence as he never had another woman's.

His thoughts turned back to her offer. No matter how he turned the situation over in his mind, he couldn't think of another solution that would immediately quiet the swirling rumors. Even if he refuted the playboy angle most outlets were running with, the news vultures would descend in bigger numbers on any sighting of him with a prospective wife. Whether the women on the prime minister's list would even want to be seen with him right now was another question. Yet the issue of how people perceived him paled in comparison to the very real threat of companies pulling out of Kelna because they doubted his ability to lead.

An issue that could be solved, at least temporarily, by one simple proposal. A proposal he would have to run by the prime minister and reassure him the engagement would be for appearances only until the press coverage died out. Then he and Madeline could part ways, her with her reputation intact and her firm still on the job, he with the confidence of his country and the investors helping it flourish.

But will you be able to let her go?

He'd given into weakness not once, but twice now where Madeline was concerned. If he agreed to her offer, what was to say he wouldn't make the same mistake a third time? What if he fell for her, truly fell, but still had to let her go?

The sun rose from behind the mountains, glimpses of the orange orb glowing behind sharp peaks still capped with snow. A wind whispered across the pine forests below and made the treetops sway. Beyond the forest lay another town, Drago Selo. He could see the red roofs, imagine the people already up and bustling about the small farming community.

So many people who depended on his family.

Who, in a short time, would come to depend on him. Whether he could keep his heart safe meant nothing compared to their well-being and future.

He turned from the window and dialed Dario's number. He had decided.

Madeline plucked at a piece of toast on the tray that had been brought to her room. Eviana had stopped by just after she'd gotten back. Instead of being angry, she'd been incredibly kind, offering to order Madeline breakfast and keep her company. She'd also threatened a variety of creative punishments on the photographer who had taken the lurid photo and managed to tease a reluctant smile from Madeline. The reserve Madeline had observed before had completely disappeared, revealing a sweet young woman beneath who, in another life, Madeline could have been very good friends with.

When the food arrived, Eviana had sensed that Madeline needed time alone. She'd given her a tight hug and a recommendation to not go into a meeting with anyone in the public affairs office unless Eviana was present.

"They mean well," Eviana had said with a wrinkle of her nose, "but they can be overbearing."

The reminder of the damage Madeline had managed to inflict with her thoughtless actions had sent her back into a state of numbness. It was the only way she was managing to make it through the morning without breaking down and crying. The one time she'd tried to settle into the comfort of a plush chair and draw, she'd ended up running the pencil in a circle over and over again until she'd worn the pencil down to a nub.

Her phone had been blowing up with calls and texts from family and friends. Her brothers' and sisters' messages had ranged from curious and excited to one threatening damage to Nicholai's person for daring to drag Madeline into the international spotlight. That last one, from her youngest brother, Cliff, had made her smile despite the gravity of the situation.

Her mother had left a voicemail, the soft voice bringing both comfort and shame.

"Darling, call when you can. I'm worried about you." A lengthy pause. *"Don't let someone take advantage of you. You don't need a man to be happy. You're enough."*

She could only imagine what this was doing to her mother. Madeline's biological father had met her mother at the diner where she had worked in college, convinced her to give up her schooling and marry him. Madeline remembered him being handsome with a charming smile and a quick joke.

Qualities, her mother had told her in later years, which had blinded her to his flighty nature, his inability to hold down a job or provide for the family he said he had wanted. They'd moved five times before Madeline had started school, usually because her father had helped himself to the rent money for some get-rich scheme or to travel somewhere under the guise of picking up work.

But her mother had fought her way out of it, had gotten a divorce and made her own way with Madeline and her sister Greta. She'd told Madeline more than once that she had thought Father was the answer to what had been missing in her life at the time.

"A dangerous way to think, Maddie. Never let someone else be the answer to your happiness."

She blinked back hot tears. At first, when she'd started dating Alex, she'd enjoyed his company. Then, as their relationship had deepened, she'd thought herself in love.

Yet, as the warning signs had started to show, from Alex's intolerance of her work schedule to his irritability over trivial things, she had brushed them aside. She'd wanted the wedding, the marriage, the kids and the house with the yard. She'd wanted a dream so badly she'd nearly let the rest of her life become a nightmare to achieve it.

Slowly, she uncurled her fingers and let the mangled bread fall onto the plate. She didn't know the first thing about being in a relationship, let alone with a prince. Not that Nicholai had asked her to be in a relationship. While they hadn't discussed the explicit details of what his future queen would do, he had agreed with her brief assessment when they'd talked in the alcove on her first visit to Kelna. The future queen would be needed here.

The rehashing did little to assuage her damaged pride. Nicholai's emphatic rejection of her idea had hurt. She hadn't made the offer lightly. But she had felt responsible for her role in the debacle. She'd been the one to invite Nicholai to dance, had most definitely kissed him back. Forge losing the contract of a lifetime because of one moment of indiscretion made her sick. Add in the possibility of Kelna's meteoric rise falling apart because she'd kissed the Kingdom's heir and she felt so heavy she could barely sit upright.

She glanced at her phone again. Thankfully, no one from Forge had reached out yet. Given that the sun had barely been up for an hour, they probably wouldn't learn of her mistake for some time yet.

And getting fired because of me.

Miserable, she moved over to the bed and flopped down, curling around her pillow and hugging it tight. The underlying thought that had been circulating since Nicholai had rejected her now rose to the surface. She couldn't do anything to help Nicholai. But there was one thing she could do to help her team. The people who had supported her through thick and thin.

Resign from Forge.

Her throat tightened as she sucked in a shuddering breath. It would kill her. She'd worked so hard for this. Her job had become her life, especially in the last year. She'd chosen it over Alex.

The right choice. And now I'm going to lose it all.

She would eventually find work. But the scandal would follow her for some time. Kissing a client was not exactly a résumé enhancer. She could strike out on her own. Except how many clients would want to work with her? Even if they did, she was still relatively new. Yes, she was confident in her skills. But she still had a lot to learn.

Doesn't matter.

It wasn't fair for everyone else to lose their chance at an assignment that could catapult their careers into stardom. Resigning was the right thing to do.

Why, she thought as she closed her eyes against a hot sting of tears, *is the right thing so damn hard sometimes?*

A knock sounded on her door.

"Not now," she called.

The door swung open. Startled, she sat up in bed as Nicholai stepped inside. She barely stopped her mouth from dropping open as he shut the door.

"I would like to take you up on your offer."

This time she wasn't able to stop her lips from parting in shock.

"But…you said—"

"I changed my mind."

"Just like that? In twenty minutes?"

"Does your proposal still stand?"

My proposal.

Heat flamed in her cheeks. Although the situation was entirely different, she had, in fact, proposed to a prince this morning. Cautious hope swirled inside her even as she kept an iron grip on her pillow.

"It does."

Nicholai exhaled a harsh breath that sounded more like accepting something disdainful versus a sigh of relief.

"All right. A representative from our public affairs office will be down in twenty minutes to brief you on the official story."

"Official story?"

"Yes. How we met, our whirlwind romance, et cetera."

Her brief moment of relief flickered and died. An underlying sense of nausea crept in.

"Why not just keep it simple? That we met in Paris—"

"We will. But we need to make sure our stories match." He ran a hand through his thick hair. "I'll drop by after the people from wardrobe come by and we'll discuss terms—"

"Wardrobe? What are you talking about?"

"We will hold a press conference at eleven to announce our engagement."

The floor dropped out from under her. "What?"

"It's best to get ahead of the story as soon as possible. The quicker we address it and perform for the cameras, the sooner we can get back to normal."

The nausea grew. How had she gone to bed with the bittersweet memory of their dance and woken up to this horrid hell that had taken the second-best kiss of her life and turned it into tabloid journalism for the world to consume?

Somehow, she forced a smile to her lips. "Of course."

Nicholai gazed at her for a long moment, as if he was waiting for her to say something else. Humiliated and suddenly exhausted, she remained silent.

He stood and moved to the door, pausing just before he went out.

"Thank you, Madeline. I owe you."

The nausea pitched into her throat. She nodded once, kept her face devoid of expression until the door closed behind him.

And then she broke down, letting her tears fall silently down her cheeks.

CHAPTER NINE

MADELINE TRIED NOT to wrinkle her nose as she looked down at her dress. The public affairs representative had picked out a black dress with sleeves down to her elbows and matching black heels. The rep had called it dignified, posh.

Madeline thought she looked like she was going to a funeral.

Might as well be.

The meeting had been hideous. The rep had obvious loyalties to the crown, loyalties that came out in clipped responses and hardly any eye contact. If this was what the rest of the world was going to think, that some upstart American had managed to snag herself a prince and drag him through the mud, then her time as the supposed fiancée of Prince Nicholai Adamović was going to be unpleasant.

She glanced down at her bare ring finger. The one detail that no one had mentioned. For the most part, the rep had emphasized keeping her mouth shut during the press conference and only speaking if Nicholai prompted her. Otherwise, "His Highness" would field all inquiries. When Madeline had asked why, the rep had responded that he had experience, whereas Madeline didn't.

The public affairs version of "sit down and shut up."

Her hair had been styled into an elegant French braid. Tiny drops of pearl adorned her ears. She looked very proper and put together.

Very much not herself.

Her phone had continued to blow up with messages, especially after the palace had announced a press conference with Prince Nicholai and Miss Madeline Delvine with some "exciting news." Shortly after eight, her team started texting her, too. Julie had been cautiously congratulatory. Andrew's simple statement of his being available if she ever needed to talk had signaled he knew more was going on. J.T. had actually stopped by to check on her and tried to pepper her with questions until the public affairs rep had stopped by and politely but forcefully escorted him out. The worst had been Chris, congratulating her and apologizing if he ever came on too strong.

How had this spiraled out of control so quickly?

The dress seemed to tighten about her ribs. Madeline stared at her reflection.

Sighing, she turned away from the mirror. She knew what the Public Affairs Department was going for. No hint of scandal. A united front that emphasized decorum and all the values that had been called into question by hers and Nicholai's midnight make out session.

It was, she kept reminding herself, all for show. In a month, maybe two or three, they'd probably make some quiet announcement about how they'd realized they were no longer suited and would part ways. Given that she was playing out the biggest lie of her life, it shouldn't have mattered that she was lying yet again in the way she presented herself.

Except it did matter. She felt like she'd slipped back into her past, into mistakes that had nearly swallowed her whole. She had started to acquiesce to some of Alex's requests in the months leading up to their breakup. Little things, like wearing a slightly longer dress, or toning down the red lipstick she preferred to wear when she went out. The more she stood up to him on things regarding her career, the more he had pushed her on things she thought of at the time as mundane. Small requests that he had phrased as perfectly reasonable and, in her attempt to mitigate some of her guilt about how much time her career demanded, she had said yes to.

She'd sworn never to do it again. To give up her independence for a man. To be someone she wasn't.

Yet here she was, once again playing a role.

Suddenly frustrated with herself, she unzipped

the dress and let it pool at her feet in a black, shapeless mess. Most of the gowns the representative had brought to her this morning were from a high-end boutique in Lepo Plavi, a shop that catered to the wealthy vacationers taking advantage of the Dalmatian Coast's sunshine and seascape.

Even if they weren't her style, the exquisite detail and attention to design were evident. Most were black or various shades of blue.

But buried beneath the mound of clothing, was a deep emerald dress. Sleeves came down to her elbows, although the scooped back probably dipped a little lower than the Public Affairs office would have liked. The bell skirt came to just above her knees, a respectable length. She swapped out the pearls for glittering citrine orbs from her own luggage. The earrings had been a gift from her mother and stepfather when she graduated college. A matching bracelet and nude heels made her feel more like herself. Classy, sure, but with a dash of much-needed color. Accents that reminded her of her family thousands of miles away.

A knock sounded on her door.

"Come in."

Nicholai walked in. His eyes swept up and down her form.

"Hello."

"What are you wearing?"

Her back went up.

"A dress."

"They told me that you were wearing black."

"I changed my mind."

"You can't just change your mind."

She narrowed her eyes at him. "What's wrong with this dress?"

"It's too bright. Not the image we're wanting to put out today."

She cocked her head to one side. "Do you really think all the newspeople that are combing through my social media right now and looking at photos of what I normally wear are going to for one second believe that I—" she pointed to the mound of fabric on the floor "—would actually wear a black dress like that?"

Nicholai blinked, as if the thought had not occurred to him.

"If I was wearing a thigh-high dress and go-go boots, I could understand the concern. But this is a perfectly acceptable dress that covers more than enough and still feels like me."

"Except you're not you anymore." He didn't say it meanly, which almost made it worse, as though he were talking to a child who didn't understand. "You're the fiancée of a prince and the future queen of Kelna."

Madeline gritted her teeth. "I'm not changing. If that means the deal's off, then I guess the deal is off. But I will not be told what to wear again by you or by anyone."

Nicholai's face darkened. "Again?"

Madeline inwardly groaned. "It's nothing. Forget it."

"It's not nothing."

Nicholai advanced into the room, his eyes narrowing in anger.

"Alex?"

Her chest tightened. She hadn't told him about Alex. But then again, she remembered with a sigh, she hadn't needed to. That stupid article had drudged up her entire life. It was a wonder they didn't include that she'd failed Mrs. Farmer's English exam in tenth grade.

"You know what's worse than making a mistake? Having literally the whole world know that you made a mistake."

"Did he try to control what you wore?"

Her anger twisted, morphed into humiliation. She had made such a hideous mistake with Alex, making excuses for him until one day he'd pushed her just far enough to finally yank the wool from her eyes. That it had taken months of his controlling behavior to get her to leave was a thorn she had yet to pull out of her side. That, coupled with her mother's warning about not letting a man take over her life, made her current predicament embarrassing.

"He had very strong opinions."

A muscle ticked and Nicholai's jaw.

"Did he hurt you?"

"Not physically." She let out a small, strained laugh as she turned away, unable to face Nicholai.

"But emotionally, mentally, yes. He hurt me. He knew how much being an architect meant to me. He only cared more about himself, about what I could do for him, instead of being partners. And when I pushed back, he found other ways to troll, to make himself feel better by at least having a say in something." She sucked in a deep breath, then faced him, her arms crossed over her chest. "I want to help, Nicholai. I know what's on the table. But please don't ask me to lie more than I have to. I know you can't completely trust me after what's happened in the past few days. But I promise I will represent Kelna as best I can—"

"Stop right there." Nicholai stalked toward her, his eyes dark and thunderous. "I take responsibility for what happened. I followed you out into the gardens to the terrace. I kissed you."

"I kissed you back."

The atmosphere in the room changed, shifted into one of awareness.

"Yes, you did." Nicholai let out a harsh exhale. Longing flashed in his eyes, a look that pierced her heart. Then it disappeared as he regained control. It was unsettling, to see a man shift from vulnerable to a commanding leader in the span of a heartbeat.

"We both know where this is headed."

Instead of feeling strong for sticking to her priorities or relief that they were on the same page, she just felt miserable.

"Yes."

"Then we won't discuss how this started any further. It's in the past." He scrubbed a hand over his face. "There will be times during this charade that I will have to ask you to do things you don't want to do. However, knowing your history, I will endeavor to make sure that what you wear is not one of them."

"Thank you." She scrunched up her nose. "Sometimes I can be independent almost to a fault."

"Shocking."

"I will try to temper some of my usual responses."

"This life is not for everyone, Madeline. Yes, it's depicted in books and movies as being hard. But the true depth of what's required of us as royals can only be understood by people in a similar position. Not," he added, "that we don't reap benefits from it. It's one of the things I have to remind myself of when I start to feel trapped."

"Trapped?" His words from the rooftop in Paris suddenly came back. "You mentioned feeling caught between two worlds."

"Yes. The Kingdom my father ruled is very different than the one of today. In the past two years it has grown rapidly, as has the scrutiny we live under from the media and the public. The number of duties has increased tenfold. So have the expectations. I receive a life of luxury, one which I strive to be grateful for. There are times when I look at the sheer amount that needs to be done and I falter. But no matter what my wishes are, or are not, I am pledged to lead in the best interests of my people."

Floored by the level of his commitment, and stunned by the depth of her own emotional response, Madeline took a physical step back. Never had she been so moved by a man's commitment to a purpose, or really anything in his life. Alex had been dedicated to his career, yes, but so much of that had been wrapped up in the money, the prestige.

Stop. She couldn't let herself feel anything more than she already did for Nicholai. Leaving was going to be hard enough as it was.

"We'll make it through this, Nicholai."

"We will." He cleared his throat. "On that note, we need to discuss the terms of our engagement."

She nodded, suddenly exhausted. "Okay."

"I spoke with the prime minister. Aside from us, he is the only one who knows this engagement is a fake."

"Not even your dad?"

"No." Nicholai paused, then rubbed at his jaw. "He has enough to be concerned about. And my sister, as much as I love her, can't be trusted to not let something slip to the wrong person."

"If this is so hush-hush, then why did you need to tell the prime minister?"

"Because he oversees Parliament. I need the ministers' approval of my fiancée."

Madeline's jaw dropped. "What?"

"It's part of the law of our country."

"That's archaic!"

Nicholai stared at her for a long moment. Something flashed in his eyes. Disappointment? Frustration? Then it was gone.

"Perhaps. But here, it's part of the law. And he agreed to help us."

Madeline held up a hand in surrender. "Okay. I'm sorry. I didn't mean to insult your country. It's just...very different."

Nicholai nodded. "Thank you. Would two months be agreeable to you?"

Her eyes widened. "Two months?"

"Long enough for the furor to die down before we announce that we have decided to step back from the engagement."

"What would happen during these two months?"

"The first month you would stay here."

"Here? As in—" she gestured to her room "—here?"

"Yes. In Kelna." He'd settled back into his lecture mode, regarding her with a neutral gaze as if he wasn't turning her world on its head. "We need to be seen together, and regularly, to sell the engagement."

"But my work...my life back home—"

"J.T. said this was your primary project at the moment. You can work on it here. Your life in

Kansas City will be waiting for you when this is over."

"So that means Forge will stay on the project?"

At his nod, she sagged in relief. Forge wouldn't lose the contract. She could keep her job, as long as J.T. didn't kick her out for bringing all this press attention to the firm. While she didn't relish being away from her home for a month or more, there was a concrete end date to this arrangement.

Suddenly lightheaded, Madeline sat down hard on a settee. Her eyes drifted to her reflection in the mirror. Beneath the expertly applied makeup, she looked pale.

"I imagine this isn't what you had in mind when you made your suggestion."

A giggle rose up in her throat, a sound that would probably come out as hysterical. She managed to swallow it by pressing her lips together and shaking her head.

"Madeline…" He knelt before her. His handsome face was the definition of serious. "If this is too much—"

"No." *Get a grip, Maddie.* "It's overwhelming, yes. But I'll make this work."

"If you're sure?"

"I am."

"All right." He stood. "We can discuss upcoming appearances and such later. Someone will be by from Public Affairs to bring you down."

"We aren't going down together?"

The thought of another stranger, someone who would probably be judging her with every step they took, made her feel sick.

"I have to meet with several people before the conference."

"Oh." Smoothing things over, no doubt. "Okay."

He turned to leave. As he opened the door, he glanced back at her.

"You do look beautiful."

The words shot straight to her heart. For one moment, as he stood framed in the doorway, she saw the man who'd drunk wine with her in Paris. Who had waltzed her about a seafront terrace. Who had kissed her like she was the only reason he wanted to keep on living.

And this time, when the wall came down and he slid back into his role as Prince, she saw him differently. Not as someone austere and unreachable. No, she saw a man who bore the burden of an entire country on his shoulders and did so with a dignity and commitment she greatly admired.

Once the door closed behind him, Madeline pressed the heels of her hands to her eyes.

I cannot fall in love with a prince. I cannot fall in love with a prince.

No matter how many times she repeated the phrase, she feared it was too late.

CHAPTER TEN

NICHOLAI ALLOWED HIMSELF to relax a fraction. Lights flashed as cameras snapped numerous pictures of him and his bride-to-be. His opening statement, carefully composed by the Public Affairs Department, had struck the right note of contrition for last night's misstep and excitement for his upcoming engagement. That his and Madeline's romance had supposedly been a whirlwind courtship begun in Paris, and the future princess was an American from an average background, had delighted the reporters thronging in front of the podium.

So far, thankfully, no one had bothered to dive too deeply into Kelna's laws. He had almost shared them with Madeline this morning. But based on her reaction to his needing the prime minister's approval for his choice of bride, he'd decided not to. It wasn't a law he liked himself, and since Madeline would be gone in two months' time, what was the point in further upsetting her? She'd put herself out on a limb to help him and Kelna recover. If he could spare her any more unpleasantness, he would.

Although she'd held up extremely well during the conference. She'd maintained a calm expression throughout, answering briefly when questions were directed to her. When one reporter had asked where her ring was, she'd looked up at him, a momentary flare of panic in her eyes. He'd slid his fingers through hers and squeezed. A soft murmur had swept through the crowd. Belatedly, he had remembered the encouragement of Public Affairs to maintain a low level of public display.

But Madeline had drawn strength from the contact and turned to face the reporter with a sweet smile.

"I'm excited to see what Prince Nicholai surprises me with. I didn't need one to say yes to his proposal." She looked back up at him then, her gaze warm and affectionate. "It's an honor to stand by his side today."

It's just an act.

But even as he felt relief that their charade was being accepted so readily, his earlier trepidation that he would fall too hard for Madeline solidified in his veins.

"Miss Delvine?"

Madeline nodded to a silver-haired reporter with a strong blade of a nose and a pen clasped in her hand like a weapon.

"Yes?"

"Sarah Tomlin, American press. How do you feel about having your engagement unveiled to the world the day after not only having *your* picture published but that of *two* other women dancing with your affianced?"

The room fell into a stunned silence as all eyes swiveled to Madeline.

Anger surged forth. He'd known this was a possibility, been lured into a false sense of security by the first round of mundane questions. He stepped forward, opened his mouth to speak.

"I would have certainly preferred to not have that photo in the papers." Madeline's slight smile, coupled with embarrassed amusement in her voice, solicited a few chuckles from the audience. Nicholai paused. Madeline had proven herself an adept speaker during her presentation to his family. While Public Affairs wanted him to do the talking, he didn't want to silence her if he didn't have to. She was already sacrificing enough.

The reporter's lips thinned. "What about Amara Atis?" she pressed. "Surely there are questions about your sudden engagement so soon after the Prince being pictured with not one but three ladies in a single evening."

Done. Madeline was well-spoken. But they were wading into dangerous territory, where the slightest mistake could be cruelly twisted and used over and over again as a weapon. They had built up a significant amount of goodwill during the first part of the conference. One wrong word could decimate it all.

He leaned towards the microphone, ready to take over.

"My fiancé talking to another woman is not a crime."

Madeline's voice had cooled considerably. Out of the corner of his eye, Nicholai saw a Public Affairs rep trying to signal him. Indecision kept him silent. If he intervened and cut her off, what impression would people form about their relationship? While Madeline was speaking more frankly than he would, she wasn't saying anything inappropriate.

"As to Miss Atis, I understand she is a long-time friend of Nicholai. I don't understand the concern."

"When your fiancé is dancing with a woman dressed like that, it's only natural—"

"Like what?"

Nicholai could feel the tension radiating down Madeline's arm and coming through her tight grasp on his hand. His own body stiffened. *Kravgu.*

He squeezed her fingers, tried to give her a silent cue to stop while she was still ahead.

She ignored it.

"If the question is simply because of what dress Miss Amara chose to wear," Madeline said in a quiet but icy tone, "then I'm disappointed."

Another ripple flew through the room. Reporters shared shocked glances. Never before had the royal family spoken so plainly. That the new fiancée of Prince Nicholai was doing so, and at her first official press conference, would be talked about for months to come.

"Disappointed?" Sarah repeated, her teeth bared like a shark. "Don't the Kelnian people have a right to know if their prince can be trusted?"

"But he can." Madeline's voice rang out, strong and sure. "I've never known anyone like the Prince. The passion he feels for this country, the support that he pours into it. I knew when my team first met with him that the addition of a new ballroom was not a vanity project. It was something that meant a great deal to him, to his family." Her voice trailed off before she rallied again. "To answer your first question, no. I have no concerns about the Prince, nor where his loyalties lie. As for Miss Atis, I hope she knows that she is always welcome here and," Madeline added with a devilish curve of her lips, "that any further gossip about her dress focuses on how well she wore it last night."

The room erupted, more questions being shouted out as conversations took place, cameras clicked away and recorded. Nicholai stood frozen in place, barely remembering to keep a faint smile on his lips.

What had she just done? What had he just let her do? Never mind how her passionate defense of him had rocked him in a way that had made him feel like a god even as it had shaken his foundation to be so responsive to someone else's opinion. His personal reaction had no place here.

Heart thumping, Nicholai leaned into the microphone.

"That concludes the press conference for today. Thank you."

He strode offstage, Madeline's hand still clamped firmly in his. He didn't stop until they were down the hall and safely ensconced in a private reception room with the door closed behind them.

He released her hand and stepped over to a silver cart on the far side, pouring himself a cup of black coffee as he sought to get his racing thoughts under control.

"Well," Madeline said from behind him, her voice cautious, "that was interesting."

"Yes. You made it even more so."

Silence reigned behind him. He took a deep drink of his coffee, inwardly cursed as the liquid scalded his tongue.

"You're upset with me."

"A little." He turned to face her. "You had explicit instructions on how to handle the questions."

Her nose wrinkled. "The question was directed to me."

"Yes. But did you not feel me squeeze your hand?"

"I did. I thought you were encouraging me."

"No, I was trying to stop you. You can't say things like that."

Bewilderment crossed her face.

"Like what? Defending you? Standing up for Amara? Refuting the nasty insinuations from that reporter?"

"When you respond like that, all you do is give them fuel for more gossip. You took what should have been a staid, polite press conference and catapulted it into what will surely become international news once again."

He knew even as he spoke that he was going too far, letting his anger at himself for letting personal whims prevent him from stopping her meld with his disappointment at how their first event had gone. She had promised him that she would represent Kelna in the best light. And then she went rogue on a reporter.

She's never been in a press conference before, his conscience whispered inside his head. *How is she supposed to know how to respond to such a question?*

"Is the motto of the royal family to roll over and take it?"

Any voices encouraging moderation or compassion disappeared. His jaw tightened as heated anger swept through him.

"Do not dare to question my family's honor."

She drew back, her lips parted in shock at the ferocity of his words.

"So you'll defend Kelna to the death, but not your fellow man? Or in this case woman?"

"What they said was unpleasant, yes. But if I would have said anything positive, they would have brought it back to the rumors of us dating. Amara and I have been friends since university. That's it. We have never, and will never date. She's used to the media scrutiny."

"But she shouldn't be." Madeline leaned forward, her hands curled into fists as she glared at him with a disapproval that nearly penetrated his own shield of ire. "She shouldn't have her choice of dress ripped apart."

"I'm surprised you even stood up for her, given how upset you seemed last night."

Madeline stared at him like he'd grown an extra head. "I was jealous of her. But I don't know anything about her. I don't know if she's kind or friendly or funny. I know nothing other than she looked amazing in a dress that made her look beautiful and she got to dance with you. For that reporter to suggest anything about her character based on a dress that—oh, my God—showed a little bit of her back, was hideous."

Reluctant admiration filled him. As he scrambled for the right words, her shoulders slumped as her face fell.

"How could you not stand up for someone you told me is a friend?"

They stood at opposite ends of the room; their

earlier camaraderie erased by the gaping distance between their roles in life.

Finally, Madeline looked away.

"It's a good thing this engagement is all for show. Because I don't understand this life at all."

Her words stabbed him in the heart. This morning, after their conversation in her room, he'd known a moment of optimism. Even if the charade ran its course and Madeline returned to America, their arrangement had given them something he hadn't thought possible: time. Time to get to know one another, to enjoy each other's company.

But with this chasm gaping between them, knowing the depth of her disgust, there would be no time spent together other than the carefully arranged appearances by Public Affairs. What would be the point? They were from two different worlds.

Hope withered, died.

"Fortunately, you don't have to."

She flinched as if she'd been struck. Disgusted with himself and his heartless response, he reached out to her, but she turned away.

"J.T. is having some of my equipment sent back when the team returns to Kansas City tomorrow. Unless I'm needed for some other show-and-tell, I'll be in my room."

The skirt of her green dress swayed like a bell as she disappeared out the door. He wanted to go after her, to tell her that even though her response to the reporter had flown in the face of every public relations lesson he had ever received during his lifetime, her defense of him, even his friend, had meant something to him. He wanted to brush the hurt from her face, soothe her anger with a walk in the rose garden in the light of day instead of skulking around at night like they had something to hide.

He turned his back on the door and moved to the window. Those were things that a man would do for his actual fiancée. Not things a prince would do for the woman playing a role to save him from public damnation.

CHAPTER ELEVEN

MADELINE SMILED AND nodded for what had to be the hundredth time in the past forty-five minutes, as a hospital administrator walked them through a door out into the bright morning sun. She blinked just as a camera clicked and silently cursed.

Get a grip. It's the third day.

Somehow, she stretched her smile just a little wider and nodded toward the photographer before redirecting her attention to the courtyard. Pastel-colored flowers and thick bushes with velvety leaves lined the meandering walkways. Benches set into the blooms offered pockets of privacy. A small fountain babbled at the far end. Despite the two dozen people in the space, the sound of the water calmed some of Madeline's tension.

She'd been left blessedly alone the rest of the afternoon and evening following the press conference. Her solitude had been ruined early the next morning by the insistent knock of a young woman who'd introduced herself as Jelena, the new aide to the future princess.

She hadn't had time to think, much less work, since. Wardrobe fittings, endless meetings, a few minutes here and there to eat while someone rattled off an endless round of trivia. If her five-year-old self could see her now, she would seriously rethink asking for that princess dress-up set for her birthday. Being a royal, even a fake one, was exhausting.

Her eyes flickered to Nicholai as the entourage moved around the courtyard. His attention was solely focused on the hospital administrator, a slight smile playing about his lips as he nodded. More than one of the doctors and nurses they'd met had given him an appreciative glance. He really was handsome. And, based on how attentive he'd stayed throughout the tour, he was good at what he did.

She inhaled deeply, exhaled softly. Nicholai was a good leader. If nothing else came of this charade, Forge would keep the palace contract, and Nicholai would be well received as king when he took the throne. From what little she'd seen, he would do the role justice.

The subject of her thoughts glanced her way. Her breath caught in her chest as their gazes met. His eyes held a question, almost as if he were checking on her. The simple moment softened her smile.

The sharp click of a camera shutter made her smile disappear. A veil dropped over Nicholai's eyes as he looked at the photographer, then turned back to the hospital administrator. Had she imagined it all? Projected what she'd wanted to see versus reality?

Probably making sure you don't run amok again.

She had been proud of herself after the press conference announcing their engagement, had thought she had handled things well, only to be faced with that blank stare Nicholai adopted so well when he was in official mode. She had thought back over what she had said, had even forced herself to watch a couple news clips that had circulated online and still could not understand Nicholai's stance that she should have just kept her mouth shut.

But she hadn't handled their post conference conversation well, either. More of an argument, really. Her last words had been spoken out of anger and hurt. Never a good combination, and, judging by the pain she'd seen flash across Nicholai's face before he'd agreed with her, she had hurt him back.

One of the few positives to come out of the situation was that her sparring with the iron-willed Sarah Tomlin had actually been well received. People lauded the future "Cinderella princess," who hadn't been afraid to speak her mind and stand up for a fellow woman. While some traditional outlets had criticized her for speaking too plainly, others had praised her for being a fresh face amongst royalty and politicians.

At least it was good for Kelna. But judging by the way Nicholai had barely spoken to her in the days since, the good press didn't matter one way or another. In his eyes, she had screwed up. While she felt sorry for the way she'd handled his reaction, she didn't, and wouldn't, regret one thing she'd said.

In the end, it didn't matter anyway. Even if Nicholai had entertained any thoughts about pursuing a romantic relationship with her, any kind of commitment to him would mean surrendering everything she held dear. She'd almost lost herself once. She would not do so again.

She glanced around the courtyard and, seeing no clock in sight, cast a glance down at her wrist. Fifteen more minutes. Then, if she remembered correctly, they would head back to the palace, where she would have just over an hour to take a shower, change and meet Nicholai, his father and his sister for a "family tea," their first get-together since this whole debacle had begun.

A headache started to build in her temples. Her hand drifted up, then fell back down to her side as she saw another camera aimed her way.

Almost over.

She'd actually enjoyed the tour. Hearing the capabilities of the new hospital compared to the old one had been interesting. The staff had been incredibly nice, a few even shyly asking for autographs. They'd also met a couple of patients and their families, who had all been lovely. It had been fascinating, too, to see the similarities and differences between American and Kelnian hospitals.

But the cameras...everywhere she turned, there was a camera, watching her every move, documenting every blink, every wrinkle of her nose.

Nicholai had texted her last night with details about the hospital tour and a request for her to join him. She'd typed out, then deleted numerous replies before finally settling on "Sure." Not the most eloquent of responses. But every other variation, from irritated refusal to grudging apology, hadn't felt right. Simplicity had won out.

Sooner or later, though, she would have to put her foot down. Part of the agreement of her staying at the palace had included time for her to work. She hadn't touched the detail designs in days. If she went more than a day without sketching, even if it was just the view outside her window, she felt the loss like a part of her had been carved away.

At last, the tour concluded with photos with the hospital staff. As they walked out, a young couple approached, asking for an autograph. Nicholai waved off his security guards as he signed a hospital brochure. A small crowd grew, drawn by the Prince and future princess of Kelna. Napkins, scraps of paper and even a book were shoved in her face, all with requests for her signature. Even though the attention overwhelmed her, she drew strength from Nicholai at her side. He took the attention in his stride, smiling as if he were enjoying it. He crouched down to talk to some young children and returned the enthusiastic hug of an elderly woman.

At last, the crowd thinned, helped along by the quiet yet firm guidance of two security guards who cleared the way to the waiting limo.

"You're really good at this," Madeline observed as they walked down the stairs.

Nicholai smiled slightly. "Thank you. I don't get to do much of it."

"Why not?"

"Too many other official duties."

"But you like talking to people?"

"Usually. Sometimes I need solitude. I don't get much of either."

Madeline hesitated, unsure of how to phrase the thought that came to mind. She waited until the doors were shut and they were ensconced in the privacy of the limo before finally saying, "I imagine doing your work while trying to take on more is hard."

"It is. I was not prepared to take on my responsibilities as well as my father's during such a critical time for our country."

"Why not ask Eviana for help?"

Nicholai frowned. "Eviana has her own duties. I've been raised for this."

The firmness in his voice signaled the subject

was closed for discussion. As the limo pulled away from the hospital, she waited until they passed the archway over the gate before leaning her head back and closing her eyes.

"Are you all right?"

She kept her eyes closed as she nodded. "I'm used to client meetings and delivering presentations. I'm just not used to having a camera on me all the time."

Something rustled across from her.

"I've never gotten used to it."

Slowly, she opened her eyes. Nicholai was glancing through a sheaf of papers inside a leather portfolio balanced on his lap. His tone was conversational, certainly friendlier than it had been since their confrontation.

"How do you manage it?"

He glanced up, his eyes focusing on some distant thought before shifting to her.

"I know it's what best for the country. For me to be seen outside the palace. So, I do it."

"You make it sound so simple."

"It's far from simple, Madeline." He exhaled slowly. "Something I forgot when I chastised you after the conference."

That made her sit up in her seat. "Oh?"

"You had all of a few hours to prepare for something others would have had months, perhaps even years, to plan for. I was overly harsh."

"Thank you." She debated for a moment on her next words. "But you still think I made a mistake."

He closed the portfolio and set it down on the seat next to him. "I don't know what to think about your statement. The reporter was overly aggressive. Her line of questioning was inappropriate. I've been trained not to respond to such things. To date, ignoring the drama seekers has served me well. However," he added as she opened her mouth to argue, "this situation is unique. Whether or not you followed palace procedure, your response has been well received. I can't argue against the results."

She sighed. "I don't know whether to be offended or appeased."

His smile flashed, quick and unexpected, a straight shot to her heart.

"You gave a human face to our country. You did what so many times I have not done. Instead of accepting things as the way they'd always been done, even wanting them to stay the same, you did something new." He reached out then and grabbed her hand. Her breath caught. A simple act, but one that made her feel accepted. Cared for. "Not only did you stand up for me, but you stood up for Amara. It meant a great deal to her."

"I'm glad." She inwardly cursed at the hint of weakness in her tone. Nicholai had told her twice now that Amara was just a friend. Even if Amara had meant more to him at some point, she had no right to be jealous.

"Amara is a friend. She's never been anything more, and never will be anything else."

Madeline ducked her head. "It's none of my business."

Nicholai tugged on her hand, waited until her eyes met his.

"This may not be a traditional engagement. But as long as we are in this together, there's only you, Madeline."

She released a shuddering breath. "Thank you. Same. There is no one. Hasn't been in over a year."

Something flared in his gaze, something that made her feel warm inside.

"I'm glad," he said softly.

He squeezed her hand before releasing it. The loss of his touch speared through her as her fingers automatically lingered, sought him before she snatched her hand back and placed it firmly in her lap.

Oh, Nicholai.

In just one conversation, he'd swept away the tension and awkwardness and replaced it with something far worse.

Wanting. She wanted Nicholai, wanted more time with him, the possibility of something more. Wanted to get to know the man behind the crown and what inspired him to return over and over again to the role that demanded so much.

"Thank you."

Unsettled by his words and the glimpse of the personal side she'd first experienced in Paris, she looked away. Vulnerability was not something she wore well. The tumultuous early years of her life had forged her into a fiercely independent child who preferred constancy. Qualities she had maintained into adulthood, minus her brief lapse with Alex.

She liked being strong. Liked the routine of her life. Yes, what she had thought of as her Paris adventure had been exciting. But she'd flown to Europe knowing she would have her apartment to go home to. Her family and friends. Familiarity. Stability.

Nicholai, on the other hand, offered the opposite of what she was usually drawn to. His life was chaotic, a constant evolution as he pivoted from one thing to the next. She'd spent mere hours in his actual presence.

Yet he drew her in like no one else had. As the limo passed by a plaza, the limestone square surrounded by elegant pillars and archways and tourists and locals moving among a sea of umbrella-covered shops and pots of the lavender flowers she'd glimpsed in the royal gardens, she felt that tug again. A sense of belonging she hadn't experienced anywhere except home.

The limo stopped at a light. Madeline looked ahead, then did a double take as she spied the large green space up ahead, partially eclipsed by rows of pine trees on either side. Stairs built into the hillside marked the beginning of a cobblestone path that wound its way across the grass. What looked like stone statues stood at random intervals on the lawn.

"What is that?"

"The Markovic. Kelna's own *muzej*, housing historic art and several exhibitions from England, Japan and America." Pride deepened Nicholai's smile. "It opened two years ago."

Madeline eyes widened as the limo passed by. "Oh, wow."

At the far end of the lawn stood a magnificent building, at least three stories tall, with pointed arches and numerous windows stretched across the front. The vivid white of the pillars and matching trim around the arched windows offset the pale redbrick walls. Terraced stairs swept up from the lawn to the main doors, wooden behemoths at least ten feet tall.

"It reminds me of the Nelson back home."

"The museum your stepfather took you to?"

Surprised and touched that he remembered, she glanced at him. "Yes."

Nicholai glanced down at his watch. "Would you like to go?"

"To the museum?"

"Yes."

Yes! "When?"

"Tonight. I'll arrange for a private tour after the museum closes to the public."

She couldn't stop her excited smile. "Really?"

"Really. We could both use a break."

"Thank you." With her spirits lifted, she pulled out her phone and typed in the Nelson's website. "This is where I spend a lot of my time when I'm not in my office."

She held up a picture of the museum's south lawn. Green grass dominated half the image, dotted with couples strolling and posing for photos, families picnicking, and a father flying a kite with his son. The trademark shuttlecock sculptures stood out in vivid white and bright orange. On the far right, the newer addition of the Bloch Building rambled over the landscape, the frosted glass walls a modern contrast to the towering stone pillars that marked the museum's regal southern entrance.

"Are those…birdies?" Nicholai's brows drew together as his lips quirked. "Like you hit in badminton?"

She chuckled. "Yes. A husband-and-wife team designed them. They imagined the museum as a net on a badminton court. There are three sculptures on the south lawn and one on the north side."

"Interesting."

She wrinkled her nose at his dry tone. "A lot of people didn't like them when they were first installed. Thought it ruined the museum's aesthetic.

And now they're a symbol of Kansas City. Something fun that people enjoy."

He tilted his head to one side as he looked back down at her phone. "Do you think that's the most important thing for a museum housing prominent art?"

"The most important? No. Very important for a free museum that serves it community? Yes."

His lips twitched. "Touché, Miss Delvine." He pointed to the glass structure on the far right side of the picture. "Different style of architecture."

"The Bloch Building. Another bit of a scandal when it was being built."

"Oh?"

"A lot of people thought it was too modern. Didn't fit in with the rest of the architecture."

"I can see the argument."

"I can, too. Although in an odd way, I'm glad people got upset. It means it meant something to them. Architecture is art. And that's the beauty of art—everyone's allowed to have an opinion. A lot of people thought it looked like a shed or storage container."

Nicholai's lips twitched. "I see the resemblance."

"But," Madeline said as she took her phone back, "for me, I see glass. Natural light. Feeling like you're a part of the landscape. Not obscuring the original architecture, but supporting it."

"Finding a way for the old and the new to coexist."

Wincing, she remembered his reaction to the initial designs. "I wasn't trying to—"

Nicholai waved his hand. "I didn't think you were purposely saying anything, Madeline. Just an observation. You're passionate about what you do. I like that about you."

Her lips parted as warmth flooded her body.

I like that about you.

She'd imagined hearing someone say sweet things to her one day. Someone who paid attention not just to the big things, but the little things, too.

Like what museum her stepfather had taken her to on their first outing.

For the first time in what felt like forever, the thought of going home to Kansas City didn't initiate an instant feeling of contentment. Instead, it filled her with an ache at the thought of never seeing Nicholai again.

How, she thought morosely, *am I supposed to walk away from this with my heart intact?*

CHAPTER TWELVE

MADELINE'S PENCIL FLEW across the paper, leaving curves and lines of graphite. She stopped, leaned her head back and frowned. With a deft movement, she flipped the pencil about and applied the eraser with intentional ferocity.

Nicholai's lips tilted up as he watched her work. In a few minutes, they would pose for their official engagement photos. When his knock had gone unanswered, he'd suspected the reason and quietly let himself in.

It wasn't just the tumble of blond locks, carefully styled in preparation for their upcoming engagement photos, that entranced him. Although the sight did make him think, for just a moment, what it would be like to brush the hair from her neck and place a soft kiss on her skin. Nor was it just the way she nibbled on her lower lip when she concentrated on something, even if it did remind him of the last time they'd touched like lovers on the cliffside terrace.

Part of Madeline's allure was her passion. She

poured herself into her art and work. He'd witnessed it here and there since meeting her in Paris. The evening after their visit to the hospital, though, had finally given him the chance to see Madeline's talent on full display.

It had been incredible.

They'd met his father and sister for tea in his father's royal quarters. Madeline's excitement at the prospect of visiting the museum had been visibly subdued when she'd first entered his father's sitting room. But Ivan and Eviana had quickly put her at ease. By the time they'd adjourned for dinner, Madeline had been sharing stories of her upbringing in Kansas City, much to his father's amusement and Eviana's delight.

That night, they'd met one of the curators for a private tour. Madeline had made the man's day by asking intricate questions and giving him her undivided attention. When she'd asked for an hour to wander, the curator had practically stumbled over his feet to offer her as long as she'd needed.

Nicholai had made himself scarce, ambling through the European exhibit that featured paintings reminiscent of the ones hanging in many of the rooms in the palace. When he'd realized it had been over an hour, he'd gone in search of Madeline. He'd found her sitting cross-legged on a bench in front of an oil painting of the palace from the early nineteen-hundreds, chewing on her lower lip as she'd drawn. Every now and then she would look up, her dark blue eyes flitting over the painting, before returning to her drawing.

He didn't know how long he'd watched her before he'd finally approached. It hadn't been until he'd sat down on the bench next to her that she'd even noticed his presence.

"It's not finished yet," she'd told him shyly before handing over her sketch pad.

She'd drawn an elegant, pointed archway of the new ballroom she'd envisioned, with glass doors flung open. Inside, vague sketches of men and women danced. Above the arch, embedded in stone, had been a cluster of blooms he'd recognized as bellflowers.

"I'm thinking keystones above each arch. Adds a touch of that tradition you like."

His fingers had settled on the flowers. "Why bellflowers?"

"The national flower of Kelna. I saw them everywhere and asked Eviana about them."

Did any of the women on Dario's list know Kelna's national flower? Would a seemingly small detail even matter to them?

It mattered to Madeline. That it did meant something to Nicholai.

He hadn't yet had time to examine the implications of that feeling. The rest of the week had passed by in a blur. Press coverage had been positive, including one picture of Madeline looking at him in the hospital courtyard with a sweet smile on her face that had social media users swooning around the world. Every day since the tour had been filled with meetings, public appearances and preparing for the royal engagement photos. Nicholai had finally selected a ring, a silver band set with tiny diamonds and topped with a halo diamond, in preparation for the photos. Dario had paid Nicholai a personal visit when he'd learned of the photos and asked just how far Nicholai intended to take the charade. Nicholai's response—"As far as I have to for the sake of the country"—had pacified the older man.

For now.

Even if it didn't begin to address the labyrinth of tangled emotions coursing through him where Madeline Delvine was concerned.

He glanced down at his watch. He hated to interrupt her work, especially with how much time she had given him. But it had to be done.

"Madeline?"

She sat up and looked over her shoulder. "Oh." She frowned. "Am I late?"

"Not yet."

"Good." His chest warmed as she smiled at him. "I had an online meeting with the Forge team yesterday morning. The design development phase is my favorite part of a project."

She held up her sketch pad. As he drew closer, the sweet scent of jasmine teased him.

"All the details come together. The windows, fixtures, everything."

There were familiar elements, like the pointed arches and domed ceiling that he'd seen around Lepa Plavi and other Kelnian towns. Features that had always been there, that he'd taken for granted.

Unlike the first revelation, when all he had been able to see was change, he now saw the blend of old and new. Saw the way the glass walls let in the light and, as he flipped through the sketches, provided stunning views of Kelna.

"Do you like it?"

"I do."

"You can tell me if you don't like it. I've had clients use all sorts of adjectives to describe their feelings about my work."

"Then believe me when I say it's nothing like what I imagined. It's better."

Her smile grew. "Really?"

"Really." He sat down in the chair next to her. "I will never fully be a fan of the modern. But the context you gave on things like the sculptures and the modern addition to your museum, learning the reason and intentions behind it, helped me look at the designs a different way. And seeing this," he said as he looked back down at the drawing, "the ways you've incorporated Kelna into this design, makes it seem both familiar and new."

"Thank you, Nicholai. That means a lot."

"You're welcome."

She stood and smoothed out the full skirts of her dress. Ice-blue with a lacy bodice and soft folds of fabric that fell into a sweeping skirt, the dress and the woman who wore it reminded him of a classic movie star.

"Do I look royal enough?"

"You look beautiful."

Pink suffused her cheeks. "Thank you. I don't think Public Affairs was a big fan of the dress that I picked."

"They don't have to be." Nicholai held out his hand. "Something you've taught me over the last few days is that while tradition has its place, so too does change."

Madeline's lips curved up. She accepted his hand. His fingers wrapped around hers. He heard her slight inhale, saw her eyes widen a moment before she looked up at him.

Time froze. His heart thudded in his chest. It had been over a week since they'd last kissed. A kiss he never thought would be repeated, even after the announcement of their engagement. Royals did not kiss in public.

But as his gaze drifted down to her mouth, he suddenly wished there was such an occasion.

A knock on the door made them startle and draw apart.

"Your Highness?"

"Come in," Nicholai ordered.

The door swung open. Ana, one of the Public Affairs representatives, walked in and bowed her head.

"They're ready for you."

Nicholai turned to Madeline and offered his arm. "Shall we?"

Madeline swallowed hard, but accepted his arm, tucking her hand into the crook of his elbow. Tension remained thick between them as Ana led them to a balcony that overlooked one of the private coves along the sea. The photographer made quick work of arranging them in various regal poses, from standing side by side to a close-up of Madeline's hand resting on his arm, the ring on full display.

"Now smile," the photographer ordered.

Madeline made a noise that sounded suspiciously like a snicker.

"What?" Nicholai murmured out of the corner of his mouth.

"I've just never been ordered to smile in such an aggressive manner."

He couldn't have stopped the laugh even if he'd wanted to. She glanced up at him with a cheeky glimmer in her eyes.

"Perfect!"

Nicholai looked toward the photographer, who was grinning at his camera screen.

"That was excellent, Your Highness. I'll have proofs to Public Affairs within forty-eight hours."

Madeline ran a finger over the soft fabric of her skirt as the photographer packed up his equipment.

"That only lasted twenty minutes."

"The palace is known for its efficiency."

"Still," she said as she moved back and forth, making the skirt flare out about her knees, "maybe I'll just wear this in my room the rest of the day."

Inspiration struck.

"What would you say to a tour of Kelna?"

She wrinkled her nose. "I was actually looking forward to having an afternoon where I didn't have to do anything official."

"Nothing official. What would you say to a drive around Kelna? See our country beyond the conferences and corporate meetings?"

"And I still get to wear the dress?"

"Yes."

She grinned. "I'm in."

Madeline's eyes devoured the terraced hillsides of Kelna's wine country. The road they were on wound its way through clusters of evergreens, past groves of olive trees and then up a hillside covered in rambling grape vines. It had been, she thought with a lazy smile as she leaned her head back against the plush leather headrest, one of the nicest afternoons she'd spent since arriving in the country.

When they'd first left the palace, with Nicholai at the wheel of an old roadster, she'd been acutely aware of the black car trailing behind them. But as he'd driven through the streets of Lepo Plavi, taking her past courtyards, shopping districts and historic sites like a grand cathedral with a mix of Roman and Baroque architecture that had made her swoon, the car had faded from her mind. Hearing him talk about it away from the spotlight, hearing the genuine warmth and appreciation in his voice, had taken her initial passion for the country and fanned it into something more. As the city gave way to homes, and the homes to fields, Nicholai had pointed out the rolling hills, the soaring peaks of distant mountains and the hint of another city in the valley beyond.

The more she saw, the more she fell in love. They passed by a stone villa with dark brown shutters. She counted at least three terraces as they drove by.

She'd loved Paris: the sight of the Eiffel Tower, the mix of languages, the scent of freshly baked bread from a *boulangerie*. Never had she imagined living there.

But here…she could imagine waking up here. Going to work at a desk with a bank of windows that offered stunning views of the sea.

It was a strange thought, given that she had never imagined anywhere but Kansas City as home. But the beauty of this country, the incredible architecture, seeing it through Nicholai's eyes, had made her fall even more in love with Kelna.

She glanced at her fake fiancé. The setting sun highlighted his handsome profile. She'd wondered that day after the hospital tour if she'd be able to stop herself from falling for him. Each passing day had made it harder to keep her heart safe. Seeing the work he did, how he committed himself to everything he did, and how his actions contributed to a stable country that was growing and providing for its people, added to her respect and admiration.

All while pulling her closer and closer to an edge she wasn't sure she could stop herself from falling over.

She stifled a sigh and looked away. When her relationship with Alex had been falling apart, she'd had friends to talk to. Family. Her mother especially. But now, she had no one. Her family wouldn't sell her story to the press. But one innocent slip to the wrong person could erase all the work she and Nicholai had put into their arrangement.

It had been easy over the past week to maintain the secrecy surrounding their engagement. The few times she talked with her team, the conversations had been focused on work. Texting and emailing allowed her to keep distance with her friends.

The phone calls with Stacey Delvine were a different story. She knew her mother suspected something wasn't right. It didn't sit well with her that she was lying to the woman who had taught her to be independent, who had stood by her and her decision to walk away from Alex.

A few more weeks, she told herself. *A few more weeks and you can tell her everything.*

The thought didn't bolster her spirits. Rather, it sent them plummeting. The thought of leaving Kelna, of leaving Nicholai, was becoming harder and harder with each passing day. And there was the question of what would face her on the other side when they officially announced the end of their engagement. Some people would be sympathetic, sure. But she had a nasty feeling that, given the press they had received in the last few days, she would be a subject of interest for quite a while. When she was ready to move on, would anyone want to date a woman who had been affianced to an actual prince, who had not one but two supposed broken engagements?

A warm, comforting weight settled on top of her hand. Her eyes drifted down and she watched as Nicholai's strong fingers wrapped around hers. His touch instantly soothed some of the tension tightening inside her chest.

"Are you all right?"

She started to offer a glib answer. But when she looked at him, saw the genuine concern in his eyes, she opted for truth.

"Thinking about the future."

"Do you mean with your job?"

"My job. What my life will look like after this."

He squeezed her hand. "You know that we'll

do everything in our power to smooth the transition for you."

"I know." She smiled a little. "I'm going to miss this place."

His arm tensed on top of hers.

"I miss it every time I leave."

"I won't miss all the media attention. I don't understand all the protocol or the need for some things to be done the way they are. But you have a beautiful country." She thought back to the people she'd met outside the hospital, the ones who had been so excited to see their prince. There had been respect in their eyes, too, not just fawning over a celebrity. "You and your family make a difference here."

"That means something to you?"

"Of course it does. It's one of the things I love about art and architecture. I love the creative side," she said with a smile, "but I also love seeing the work we do make a difference. Like the ballroom. There's a lot of pride in Kelna. Knowing that your family is going to make an effort to include the people in events held at the palace makes the project so much more meaningful."

"I'm glad."

His voice came out rough, but when she looked at him, he was facing forward, his eyes fixed on the road.

"What are your future goals for your career?"

"One day I'd love to open my own architecture firm."

"How long will that take?"

"At least another ten years. I still have a lot to learn, and it's not exactly cheap to start up a business."

"What would you focus on?"

Warmth curled around her even as the setting sun ushered in a coolness that seeped in through the open window. Alex had never asked her about her future goals. He'd only cared about his own vision for their future, which had included a lavish house and expensive vacations. That Nicholai cared enough to ask brought about a contentment that made her relax and share more than she had planned.

"I don't want to limit myself. I've worked on libraries, houses, even a university building. I love the variety, getting to challenge myself, incorporating different styles of art with people's preferences and dreams."

"Will you always work in Kansas City?"

Her heart fluttered in her chest. A week ago, she would have said yes without hesitation. But now, as the car turned left and climbed higher still, providing the most incredible view of the valley to the west, she wasn't sure. Not only was Kelna an incredible country, but it had pushed her out of her comfort zone. Made her think about possibilities beyond the path she had always envisioned for herself.

"We'll see."

Lights appeared up ahead. As they drew closer, Madeline saw a redbrick building materialize against the backdrop of pine trees. Curved windows marched along the front, lit up from within with a golden light. Outside, a patio offered wrought iron chairs and pots overflowing with colorful blooms.

"Where are we?"

"A winery. My mother's family has owned it for over one hundred years."

Surprised, she turned to him as he pulled the roadster into a parking lot. The security car, which she had completely forgotten about, pulled in alongside them.

"That's amazing!"

"Wine is one of our top exports." He said it matter-of-factly but not without a great deal of pride. "My grandfather served as the minister of agriculture for years. Owning a vineyard was his idea of relaxing."

A hostess greeted them at the door and led them through the tasting room and out a back door, where a private terrace surrounded by grapevines awaited. String lights created a golden glow over the smooth stones of the patio. To the east, the mountains soared up, the setting sun painting the slopes with hues of orange, pink and violet. To the west, the terraced hillside was brushed with the darkness of encroaching night. A sommelier joined them on the patio and offered several wines for tasting. After Madeline requested a rosé and Nicholai settled on a port, the sommelier poured and left them alone on the patio.

He leaned back in his chair. "Tell me about your life."

"My life?"

They were interrupted by a waiter who came to take their food orders. Once he left, Nicholai pressed her.

"Back home. What's it like in Kansas City?"

"I already told you some in Paris."

"You did. Tell me more."

So she did. She told him about the jazz club that catapulted one back to the Roaring Twenties, the distillery where she'd bottled gin in college, the various districts with their unique shops and venues. The botanical gardens to the east of the city that blended prairie with forest. The soaring tower of the museum honoring those who served in the Great War.

"Paul got my sister Greta and me hooked on BBQ. You'll have to try it if you ever travel there."

"I will." He cocked his head to one side. "You mention Paul a lot. May I ask what happened to your birth father?"

She glanced down at her wineglass.

"I apologize. That was rude—"

"No. No, it's just… I rarely talk about him. Sometimes I forget he was ever a part of my life." She blew out a harsh breath. "My father flitted from job to job, sometimes disappearing for days and weeks at a time. We moved five times before I started kindergarten, usually because a check bounced or we were evicted for nonpayment. When he was gone, Mom was working herself to the point of exhaustion, but we were always happier." She ran a finger up and down the stem of her wineglass, her eyes distant as she revisited the past. "Those years shaped me. I love my work and where I live. But I also like the familiar. The knowing that I always belong somewhere."

"Where is he now?"

"I don't know. I have a vague memory of him coming back, sitting at the breakfast table, and saying something about needing more money." Her lips curved up. "What I do remember, vividly, is my mother packing up our belongings and stuffing them into a rusted tank of a car. We moved to Kansas City. Mom found work fairly easily, first as a waitress, then a bartender, and then a restaurant manager. She met Paul there."

"And they lived happily ever after in a home along the river where you watched the fog roll in."

Her eyes crinkled at the corners as she smiled. "Yes. The rest of my childhood was a happy one. They set the bar high."

She leaned back in her chair, her eyes drifting up to the sky for a moment before her gaze returned to his. Her expression reminded him of Paris, made his heart leap as she looked at him with such warmth it made him long for endless nights like this.

"Thank you for this, Nicholai. Tonight, and the museum trip... I needed these breaks."

"You're welcome, Madeline." He held up his glass.

"What are we toasting to?"

He paused for a moment. "How about the future?"

She smiled and held up her own. Their glasses clinked. "To the future."

CHAPTER THIRTEEN

NICHOLAI SHOOK HANDS with Arthur Brandon, head of Brandon Consulting and one of the primary benefactors of Kelna's recent economic fortunes.

"We are very pleased with what we've seen, Your Highness."

Arthur smiled. The gesture was cold, edged with a steely strength that had catapulted the finance consultant to the head of a global firm that could make or break fortunes in a matter of hours. Arthur's reputation for rigid control also made him very selective about who he worked with. Any sign of risk and he had no problem severing ties and moving on to his next project. With a significant percentage in one of the shipping companies that would be utilizing Kelna's port, he wanted to ensure its success.

"Thank you, sir."

Arthur turned his attention to Madeline. His face softened just a fraction.

"And you, Madeline. It's nice to finally meet the future princess who's caused such a stir."

"For the right reasons this time, hopefully," Madeline replied with a slight smile.

Arthur's lips formed into something reminiscent of an actual grin. Nicholai blinked. He wouldn't have believed it if he hadn't seen it with his own eyes.

"Everyone is entitled to a mistake here and there," Arthur said.

But his eyes flickered to Nicholai, a hint of warning in the sharp depths. Nicholai kept his expression neutral, not deigning to play the man's game of control. Yes, losing Brandon Consulting's investment would be a huge setback. But it would not be the end. Kelna was too strong to be at the mercy of one man.

Nicholai glanced down to see Madeline's lips part, as if she were about to utter a retort. But then she pressed them together into a thin line.

"Thank you."

"Until our next meeting then." Arthur bowed his head to Nicholai. "Your Highness. Ma'am."

Madeline waited until the door closed behind Arthur before spinning around, her eyes snapping fire.

"That man is awful."

Nicholai chuckled. "Thank you for not saying that in front of him."

Madeline wrinkled her nose. "I wanted to say that and more. But I'm working on my diplomacy.

I could see that self-righteous jerk pulling all of his financial support."

"He's been known to do that over far less."

Madeline's hands moved over the cups and saucers, pouring tea in one and coffee in the other. It had been two days since their winery adventure. Business had kept him from spending any more time with her. So when Arthur's team had requested a meeting with both the Prince and his fiancée, Nicholai hadn't even regretted that he would have to meet with the pompous financier. Not if it meant more time with Madeline.

He watched as she added a dash of milk and a small spoon of sugar into the coffee, stirring it before she brought it to him. The moment, simple yet domestic, struck him. The few women he had dated hadn't brought him coffee, much less taken the time to notice how he preferred his.

"I'm assuming Kelna does not have the financial resources to tackle all this development alone."

"No. But we will become financially independent. Until then, we play the game."

Her hands cradled her cup, as if she were drawing strength from the heat seeping through the porcelain.

"It seems like a dangerous, ugly world to me. But then I think back to some of the contracts, some of the people we've done business with." She blew on the surface of her tea, ripples chasing each other across the surface. "It's not as different as I thought. Putting on one face to convince someone to pick our firm. Putting on another to get money from an investor."

Shoulder to shoulder, they gazed out over Lepa Plavi. The bell tower stood tall and proud over the city. The bell had been used for centuries to warn of everything from an invading army to an approaching storm. History, culture, so much uniqueness that made his country home.

Beyond the city, the crane he had seen from the window of the plane when he'd flown into Kelna with Madeline and her team nearly two months ago broke the peacefulness of the landscape.

As if sensing how much the site of the construction bothered him, Madeline leaned her head against his shoulder.

"Why does it bother you so much?"

"It's the first decision my father truly put in my hands. There's responsibility. I always thought of myself, too, as modern. Forward-thinking." He nodded to where bulldozers moved back and forth shoving heavy mountains of rock to the side to make way for the new. "The buildings that were there were old, abandoned storefronts and an old hospital that we had once thought about turning into apartments. Nothing significant."

"Still, a part of your country's history. Change can be bittersweet."

"It can. Being beholden to so many and their goodwill makes the change heavier."

"And adds more responsibility you hadn't anticipated."

He gave in to desire then, slid an arm around her waist and pulled her close, taking strength from the simple contact. The beautiful peacefulness of being able to touch the woman who seemed to understand him like no one else, who had shown up when he'd needed her most, calmed him even as it warmed his heart. A woman who continued to stand strong and rise to the challenge of meetings and public events and unwanted media attention with increasing grace and confidence.

He breathed in, savored the light floral scent that clung to her hair.

"It is a bit jarring," she finally said as she continued to watch the frenzy of construction.

"The finished port will be similar to your design of the ballroom. Same coloring and stone style as Lepa Plavi. Blending of old and new."

She was quiet for a long moment. "And you truly like the ballroom design?"

He smiled against her hair. "It's grown on me."

She laughed. "Seriously, though."

"I do like it, Madeline. Not what I expected. But the more I've seen it, the more I know it will be an excellent addition to the palace. It will be the kind of space we can host guests and visitors with pride. The views will be unbeatable."

The morning after their trip to the winery, he'd walked out to stand in the spot where the new ballroom expansion would reach. Picturing the views from the glass walls had made him further appreciate the work Madeline had done, the vision she had created.

The door behind them burst open.

"Your Highness!"

An aide rushed into the room, tears streaming down her face. Fear exploded in his chest.

"The King?"

"No, sir. A bridge collapse. A school bus was on it—"

Nicholai was running for the door before she'd finished her sentence. He felt Madeline just behind him.

"There's nothing you can do," he said over his shoulder.

"Don't give me that." Madeline followed him through the maze of hallways to the grand hall, quickening her pace to keep up with his determined jog. "I'm not just going to stay here at the palace. There must be something I can do."

He glanced down at her, at the determination on her face.

"All right."

For the second time in two weeks, the limo made the journey to the hospital, this time at a more rapid pace. *The hospital's new trauma center*, Nicholai thought grimly as the car pulled up to a private entrance, *is about to be tested.*

They were rushed inside by palace security. A hospital security guard guided them to an administrative wing just down the hall from the emergency room. A grim-faced woman met them in the hall.

"Your Highness. Miss Delvine. I'm Marta Horvat, one of the hospital administrators."

"An aide briefed me on the way in. The bridge just crumbled?"

"Yes, sir. Fortunately, the drop was only ten feet or so. Other bridges in the area are over thirty to forty feet. It could have been much worse."

Nicholai steeled himself. "How many casualties?"

"Twenty with minor injuries. Three will require surgery, and two are in critical condition."

"But no deaths?" Madeline asked quietly.

"Not so far, ma'am."

Madeline sagged in relief as the pressure eased in his own chest.

"Thank you. Miss Delvine and I will be staying on for a while."

"I'll have the hospital security team—"

"No." Nicholai softened his order with a hand on Marta's shoulder. "Your team needs to focus on your patients and your staff. Don't worry about us. Pretend like we're not even here."

Marta sucked in a shuddering breath. "Thank you, Your Highness."

Nicholai waited until the woman was out of earshot before he turned to Madeline.

"This isn't going to be easy. There's the potential..." His voice trailed off, not even wanting to contemplate the possibility of what awaited them in the emergency room.

"I know." She reached up, cupped his face in her hands. "I know that this engagement is only for show, and temporary at that, but while it lasts, I'm not just going to show up for the nice and pretty events. I'm here to help you." Her hands tightened. "Let me help you."

He gave in, dipping his head to kiss her. It wasn't the sweet romance of their kiss in Paris, nor was it the frustrated passion that had brought them together on the seafront terrace. This was desperate, a need to connect before they walked into the unimaginable. His arms came around her, hugged her close, as she kissed him back.

A woman's voice cut into the moment through a loudspeaker in the ceiling, speaking first in Croatian, then English.

"Ambulance arriving, ambulance arriving. Status critical."

Nicholai and Madeline broke apart. Her eyes glinted bright in the light of the hallway, but her jaw was determined, her shoulders thrown back as if readying for battle.

"What first?"

"I need to find out what happened. If there're

any risks to other bridges in the area." The sound of a distant sob came from the doors leading to the emergency room. "I need to meet with the families, too."

"What if I see the families while you talk with someone who knows what happened? Then come back here and meet with the families."

Some of the tension eased from his shoulders. He was used to doing things alone, especially after Ivan's illness, to dictating and trying to get through his priorities as quickly and efficiently as possible. The novelty of having someone to share the burden with, someone he trusted, was an unexpected gift.

"Let's go."

Five hours later, Nicholai could barely stand. So far, every patient was stable, even the driver who had borne the brunt of the damage when the bus had driven off the edge. After traveling out to the site and meeting with emergency crews and the Transportation Division, he'd returned to the hospital. Eviana had joined Madeline while he'd been at the scene of the accident. Together, they had already met with most of the families. The emotions of the people he'd met with ranged from shock and disbelief to bone-deep anger. Feelings he certainly did not begrudge them as initial facts started trickling in.

The bridge, it seemed, had been in desperate need of repair for months. The inspector responsible, however, had decided to write the bridge off as passing inspection instead of doing his job. Nicholai had already consulted with the police to ensure his arrest would be swift. Public Affairs was putting a conference together for later that afternoon, one that would be presided over by the King, Nicholai, the head of transportation and a representative from the hospital.

Nicholai rubbed the bridge of his nose. Orders had already been placed for new inspections on every bridge the inspector had been responsible for in his three years on the job. It amounted to nearly a third of Kelna's bridges. Nicholai had agreed with the transportation director's decision to order emergency closures, which would create traffic nightmares for a good portion of the Kingdom.

Better to have a traffic jam than any more accidents or, God forbid, deaths.

Nicholai glanced up and down the hall. The palace had stationed security guards at every entrance. Several others walked through the halls, ensuring that the only people allowed in or out were medical personnel or families of the victims. Not just for Nicholai, Eviana and Madeline, but to provide the families with much-needed privacy as hordes of news vans and reporters gathered outside the hospital.

He frowned as his eyes swept the chairs and couches in the waiting room. Madeline had been by his side for the past two hours, hugging crying mothers and fathers, consoling siblings and listening to the shouts of one particularly furious parent that had nearly resulted in security intervening.

She had stood up to it all. Perhaps she had just needed a break.

"Are you looking for the Princess?"

An older woman dressed in blue scrubs with fatigue etched into her dark brown skin, stopped next to him. He started to correct her use of the title, then stopped. A trivial detail, especially given what Madeleine had done today.

"Yes. I assumed she was taking a break."

A small smile crossed the nurse's face.

"No, sir. I'll take you to her."

She stopped outside a door marked with a patient number. After a gentle knock, she opened the door and poked her head inside. She glanced back at Nicholai and put a finger to her lips.

"They're still sleeping."

Nicholai walked in. Then stopped, floored by the sight in front of him.

Madeline sat in a chair in the corner. A little girl was curled up under a blanket on her lap. Her head rested against Madeline's shoulder, tousled curls covering most of a white bandage across her forehead. Their chests rose and fell with their deep, even breathing.

The little girl whimpered in her sleep. Madeline started, her eyelashes fluttering as her arms tightened around the child. The girl settled and both slipped back into sleep.

Tenderness flooded him. He had thought occasionally of having children, but it had never been something he'd paid particular attention to. It was inevitable, of course, for ensuring the line of succession.

But as he watched Madeline and the little girl sleep, he saw a future in stunning clarity. One with Madeline as the mother to his children, showering them with unconditional love as she brought a much-needed dose of normalcy to the chaos of living in a royal household.

Nicholai barely covered his start of surprise as he realized the nurse still stood behind him. He racked his brain.

"This is the girl whose parents are out of the country?"

The nurse nodded. "The family friend who was watching her had to leave to go pick up her own children. Your fiancée offered to stay, Your Highness."

Nicholai nodded, trying to fight past the tightness in his throat. "Thank you."

"I hope it's not too forward of me to say, but you chose well, sir."

Her words stole some of his contentment as she exited the room. He hadn't chosen at all. It had been Madeline who had put forth the idea, Madeline who had risen not once, not twice, but now three times, giving her all to their fake engagement, and who, with her fierce independence and kind heart, was winning over not only his country but the world.

He slipped out, but not before stopping to glance back. Dark shadows covered the pale skin beneath Madeline's eyes. The bun at the nape of her neck had come loose, wisps of hair sticking out at odd angles.

She had never looked more beautiful to him than she did in that moment.

He knew, as he closed the door behind him, that he would not be the only one who would mourn when their engagement came to an end.

CHAPTER FOURTEEN

MADELINE WOKE TO hushed whispers in the hospital room. The weight of Mina on her chest registered a moment before she would have stood.

Slowly, she opened her eyes. A couple stood on the other side of the room. The woman, with the same ringlets as Mina, except in a darker shade of blond, had her arms crossed tightly over her chest. A tall, heavier man stood next to her; a protective arm wrapped around her shoulders. Nicholai and the nurse who had brought Madeline in stood talking with them in hushed tones.

As if sensing her awaking, Nicholai's eyes shifted to hers. The emotion burning in his gaze hit her hard. Challenging as it had been, the afternoon had brought them closer together. Her respect for Nicholai, as well as her appreciation for the role he served, had deepened even more. Now she better understood the pressure Nicholai put on himself, how seriously he took his role.

"Oh." Mina's mother hurried over, her eyes focused on her daughter's sleeping form. "Thank you, Your Highness. For caring for our little girl."

"Oh, I'm not—"

"Mommy?"

"Mina!"

Mina launched herself from Madeline's lap into her mother's and father's arms. Madeline barely managed to blink back her own tears as she got to her feet and set the blanket aside.

"How can we ever repay you for being here when we weren't?" Mina's mother asked as she clutched Mina to her chest and rocked her daughter back and forth, tears slipping down her cheeks.

"By continuing to be the kind of parents that obviously love their daughter very much."

Her words made Mina's mother cry harder as Mina's father shook her hand and then pulled her gruffly into a hug. Nicholai kept a watchful eye on the man until he released Madeline. The man echoed his wife's words of thanks and then joined his family on the sofa.

She and Nicholai exited the room, leaving the united family in peace.

"How long was I asleep?"

"At least an hour, possibly more."

"I'm sorry. I left you to deal with all of it alone—"

"No."

Nicholai took her hands in his and stepped close. She knew the display of affection was discouraged by protocol, making his touch even more meaningful.

"You comforted a little girl in her hour of need. You were doing exactly what you should have been." His expression darkened. "If I had known our agreement would lead to this, I never would have agreed to it."

"I would have." She looked around the bustling corridor, at the slightly calmer expressions of the families now comforted in the knowledge that their children were at the very least safe. "This has really opened my eyes to what you and your family do."

"Speaking of," he said, as he released her hands and began to walk down the hallway with her at his side, "we have another press conference this afternoon. Eviana is still visiting with some of the other families, but she will join us at the podium to present a united front. My father's doctor advised against him coming to the hospital, but he will lead the press conference." He looked down at her. "Will you come with us?"

"Are you sure you trust me to keep my mouth shut?" she asked with a sassy grin, trying to lighten the somber mood.

He stared at her with complete seriousness. "Completely."

Touched, she swallowed hard and nodded.

"Good. They've arrested the inspector who falsified documentation saying that he had performed a complete inspection last year."

"What?" Outrage filled her as a nurse wheeled a child by in a wheelchair, his leg wrapped from ankle to knee in a thick bandage.

"He will be punished to the fullest extent of our laws. We've also demanded emergency inspections on all the bridges he was responsible for during his time with the transportation department. This will not happen again."

She believed him, knew that he wouldn't stop until he had ensured his country was safe.

A thought hit her.

"Nicholai…"

"What is it?" he prodded gently when she fell silent.

"The ballroom. It's not right moving forward with it right now."

"The money covering those projects comes from two different funds. But I see your point." He thought for a moment, then nodded. "I'll have to verify with my father and Eviana, but I think you're right. It would be in poor taste to continue right now."

"Perhaps when the new bridge is up and the others have been inspected?"

Nicholai gave her a small smile. "I know the thought of a royal life holds no appeal for you. But you would make an excellent princess."

He turned and left her staring after him, at a loss for words. Was Nicholai suggesting that he wanted to turn their performance into something more? Something that would result in her actually accepting his ring as the future queen of Kelna?

Two weeks ago, her answer would have been an immediate no. But as she watched Nicholai bend down and speak with the grandparents of one of the victims, she no longer knew the answer to that question.

The next week passed swiftly. The press conference was well received, as was Madeline's idea of postponing the ballroom project. Ivan had proven that his illness, while devastating, could not stop him from rising to the occasions that required his leadership, with he and the other leaders of the various agencies that had responded receiving accolades for their quick action.

In the wake of the immediate arrest of the inspector, coupled with Nicholai and the Transportation Department's quick action regarding the remaining bridges and Ivan's immediate pledge to cover any and all medical and other associated costs of the victims and their families, the reception had been surprisingly positive. So, too, had been the immediately proposed policy that would add a second inspection to all future inspections.

It hadn't hurt that the kindly nurse who had shown Nicholai to Mina's room had snapped a photo of Madeline and Nina fast asleep, one that she had shared privately with Mina's mother. The mother had then shared it on her social media with a heartfelt thanks to the Prince and Princess for stepping up in her absence. The photo had spread like wildfire, catapulting Madeline back into the spotlight.

Nicholai pushed back from his office desk and moved to the window. Madeline had made several more visits to the hospital and had sat in on meetings with Nicholai. Doing everything an actual fiancée would.

Making him wish more and more that this could be an actual engagement.

Then had come a true test for their fake engagement. J.T. had requested Madeline's presence back in Kansas City for a couple of days to meet with the team and the structural engineer. Saying yes had been one of the hardest things he'd done in a long time. When Madeline had left, she'd hugged him, but they hadn't repeated their kiss from the hospital. A fact that now pricked the skin between his shoulder blades and created a restlessness he couldn't ignore.

He was falling in love with Madeline. He'd known it was a possibility, had told himself he would be able to hold up if it happened and carry on.

But more and more, he didn't want to. Unfortunately, his own wants paled in comparison to the fact that Madeline was uncomfortable with royal life. That, and her career, were steep obstacles. Nor the issue of the requirements of the Marriage

Law. Numerous problems he didn't have any solutions for.

His cell phone rang.

"Yes?"

"Your Highness." Charles, the chief public affairs officer, sounded grim.

"What is it?"

"Miss Delvine's ex has given an interview. It was published in a local Kansas City paper this morning."

A fury unlike any Nicholai had ever known pounded through him.

"What did it say?"

"It could be far worse. But he makes certain intimations about his and Miss Delvine's relationship."

Nicholai moved back to his desk and typed in Madeline's name. The most immediate results still focused on her and Mina in the hospital, as well as her involvement in the aftermath of the bridge collapse. But a couple links down, he saw the article in question.

Exclusive Interview with Future Princess Madeline Delvine's Ex-Fiancé

"Has anyone spoken to her yet?"

"No, sir."

He hung up. Why, of all weeks, did her weasel of an ex have to pick this one to crawl out of his hole and drag her name through the tabloids? He wanted to go to her, to hold her and reassure her that it would all be okay. But she was thousands of miles away.

He dialed her number.

"Hey." The waver in her voice told him she'd already seen the article.

"Are you all right?"

"I've been better."

Guilt punched him in the gut. Madeline had hinted that her ex had been manipulative. To him, it had sounded like abuse.

"I'm sorry, Madeline."

"It's not your fault my ex is a jerk."

"No. But what were the chances that he would have come back into your life if not for this?"

"I don't know."

The weariness in her voice alarmed him more than anything else could have in that moment. She had stayed strong through so much.

"What are you doing this week?"

"Hiding in my apartment. People were showing up outside the office. Reporters were calling. J.T. finally suggested I take some time off and go home."

Her misery cut him deep. To have her work cut short and her visit home tainted made him furious.

A chill crept up his spine. He was in love with Madeline, yes. But would asking her to be his lead only to misery?

Even as he felt like someone had ripped his heart out of his chest, inspiration struck. A small way that he could give Madeline a break from the chaos. Buy him more time while he figured this out. It was a selfish idea, he freely admitted.

"Meet me in Los Angeles."

A beat of silence followed, then, "What?"

"It's, what, 10:00 a.m. there?"

"Yes, but—"

"I'll charter a plane to fly you from Kansas City to Los Angeles. It'll be ready within an hour. Can you take a few days off?"

When she spoke, the smile in her voice bolstered his spirits. "J.T.'s already put me on leave. So yes."

"I'll be there as soon as I can."

Nicholai called his secretary next. Minutes later, he was walking down the hall to his father's office. He knocked before announcing himself.

"Enter."

The weakness in his father's voice made him hesitate. What was he doing? Flying off on some exotic vacation while the King struggled?

"Nicholai?"

Nicholai pushed open the door. Ivan sat behind his desk, glasses perched on the tip of his nose. Stacks of papers were arranged in neat piles on the surface.

"How are you, *otac*?"

"Alive," Ivan replied dryly. "I've had better days. But today is not the worst." He gestured to the laptop in front of him. "I assume you are here because of the story?"

"Yes."

Ivan stared down at the screen for a long moment. "Fortunately for both Madeline's sake and the country, the recent positive press only makes this young man look more like a *dupe*."

Nicholai couldn't hold back his smirk. "I can't remember the last time you cursed."

"I like Madeline. She makes you happy. And one day soon, she will be my daughter-in-law."

Nicholai's chest tightened. What had he expected when he started this charade? His first and primary goal had been to save Kelna from the fallout of his impetuous actions. He hadn't envisioned Madeline becoming so important to him, nor to his family.

But now, as the lie continued to grow, he felt ensnared by the web he'd spun.

"How is she?"

Nicholai blinked and refocused on his father. "All right. I hate that she wasn't here when the story was published."

"Why not go to her?"

"That's actually why I came." He cleared his throat. "I want to take her away. To truly give her a break from the press."

"For how long?"

"A few days."

"Do you trust your sister and me enough to leave us alone for so long?"

Even though his father's eyes twinkled as he

said it, Nicholai frowned. "I don't know why you and Eviana think I don't trust you."

Ivan's gaze darkened with sadness. "You think I don't see the burden that has been placed on you? The knowledge of what will come to be? The position that will leave you in?"

Cold fingers reached into Nicholai's chest, wrapped around his heart, and squeezed.

"It's my duty."

"It doesn't mean it's not a heavy burden to bear. I benefited greatly from my father's tutelage. I had over a decade of assuming more and more responsibility. Not a year."

"No."

Nicholai paused, allowed himself a moment of grief so deep it clawed at him, threatened to tear him apart.

And then pulled himself back together.

"I won't fail."

"I have no doubt you won't fail the Kingdom. But," Ivan added gently, "I worry you will fail yourself. It is not a weakness to ask for help, to open one's self to another. To trust them to love you at your best and your worst."

Like Madeline.

She had seen him at his worst after the first press conference. Had stood by his side through scandal, the mundaneness of everyday life and heartbreak as Kelna had faced down one of its worst accidents in years.

For better or for worse.

Vows he intended to utter within the year. Before Paris, he would have said them for the sake of his country and preserving his family's line.

But now...now he wanted to say them for all of that and more. For a woman who brought out the best in him as a leader, whom he suspected was coming to love Kelna like it was her own country.

Could he offer her enough? Would the life of a working royal sustain her the way her career did? Would he be asking too much of her?

"She is a good person, *moj sin.*"

Nicholai quelled his errant thoughts as he nodded. "She is."

"And now you must go to her." Ivan smiled at him. "Enjoy this reprieve. You both have earned it."

Guilt flickered through him as he left. He had deceived his father in the beginning because he'd thought to handle the situation of his scandalous kiss with Madeline on his own. Now he was paying the price of the lie that lay between them, of not being able to talk with his father about his evolving feelings.

Frustrated, and anxious to get to Madeline, he headed to his chamber to pack. Whatever happened during this sojourn to paradise, he was going to enjoy every last minute he could with the woman he could no longer picture his life without.

CHAPTER FIFTEEN

MADELINE PULLED BACK the gauzy curtain and stepped out onto the patio. Just below the patio, crystal clear water lapped at the stairs leading down into the lagoon. Beyond the breakers, the deep blue waters of the South Pacific stretched to the horizon.

When Nicholai had told her to meet him in Los Angeles, she'd expected a weekend getaway, perhaps a trip to California's wine country or somewhere else where they could be away from the prying eyes of the paparazzi. A car had been waiting for her in Los Angeles and whisked her away to a prominent hotel in Malibu. The penthouse had afforded stunning views of the Pacific. She'd dived into the sea of faces surrounding her and gone out for dinner at a wonderful Italian bistro, followed by a large glass of wine at a sidewalk bar.

The brief return to normalcy had been a much-needed balm for her wounded pride after Alex's article had come to light. Once again, she'd been hit with a barrage of text messages, phone calls and, worst of all, another conversation with her mother, who was growing increasingly worried about Madeline's cryptic responses to her supposed engagement.

Things were about to come to a head. She was sure of it. Even though she had sensed her and Nicholai growing closer, he had said nothing about making any changes to their arrangement. Still confused herself as to how she would reply if he asked, she had said nothing.

Coward.

She brushed that aside as she leaned against the rail and breathed in the heady mix of sea and tropics. The following morning, the front desk of the hotel had called to let her know a car would be by at 10:00 a.m. The car had taken her back to the airport, where Nicholai had been waiting next to another private jet.

When she'd seen him, she hadn't been able to stop herself from running to him and throwing her arms around his neck. Instead of stepping away or chastising her, he'd crushed her to him in a tight embrace that instantly washed away the strain of the past couple of days.

They boarded the plane, with Nicholai responding to her repeated questions as to where they were headed with an enigmatic smile. It hadn't been until the plane turned and continued out over the ocean that Nicholai had finally told her they were heading to Bora Bora.

And now she was here. On a private island resort for the world's elite who needed privacy and vacation in equal measure. Sharing a two-bedroom over-the-water bungalow with her fake fiancé.

Her bed sat on a see-through floor. With the flick of a switch, the glass would go from opaque to a window into the lagoon beneath her. Last night, she'd pressed the button that had turned on lights beneath the floor, giving her an incredible view of the sea world at night.

They'd eaten on the plane, so Nicholai had only ordered champagne and chocolate-covered strawberries as their welcome meal last night. They had sat at the mosaic-inlaid table for two, saying almost nothing and simply enjoying the novelty of anonymity in a luxurious surrounding that, two months ago, Madeline could never have pictured herself enjoying.

She glanced over at the other bedroom suite. When Nicholai had told her that the bungalow had two bedrooms, she felt like he had been waiting for her to say something. Part of her had wanted to tell him then the conflict she was feeling over her growing feelings for him versus her uncertainty about being a part of the royal family.

Except the attention she had received following Alex's interview had been yet another reminder of the intense scrutiny the people in Nicholai's world faced. Even if she could adjust to that, accept it as a part of a new life, how could she possibly give up her career? Something that meant so much to her on both personal and professional levels? Something that brought her joy? Would she come to regret what she had given up, possibly even become resentful of Nicholai and the crown?

"Good morning."

Madeline turned to see Nicholai smiling at her. In a black V-neck shirt and tan linen pants, he looked the most relaxed she'd ever seen him.

"You were thinking deep thoughts."

"I was."

"Care to share?" he asked as he joined her at the rail.

"Not at the moment." She reached over and laid her hand on top of his. "I think right now the moment calls for relaxing and indulging." She smiled up at him. "Thank you, Nicholai. This is exactly what I needed."

"I know." Regret colored his tone. "When Public Affairs told me about that article..."

Madeline tightened her fingers over his. "I'm a big girl. I didn't fully understand what I was doing when I offered to be your fake fiancée, but I still proposed it and I continued with it, even after I realized what it meant." Before Nicholai could continue down his path of self-flagellation, she nodded out at the lagoon. "We have four whole days at our disposal. What should we do?"

Nicholai's brows drew together. "I hadn't thought beyond getting here and escaping the paparazzi."

"My mother taught me that on a vacation, you

should do one thing a day. Anything more and you risk getting burned out. And always build in days for resting."

"Sounds like a wise plan."

"I have friends who go in with a full itinerary. Scheduled stops, tour guides, the works. They enjoy it. But I don't."

"Sounds like an average day to me."

She lightly nudged him with her shoulder. "So, let's change that up. Get you to relax a little."

"I'd like that, Madeline."

The sound of her name on his lips, said with caressing warmth, filled her. She resolved in that moment that, no matter what happened at the end of their vacation, she would enjoy herself and her time with Nicholai.

She walked toward the stairs leading down into the water. "Let's start with a swim."

She slid into the warm water. Nicholai joined her after changing into a pair of black swim trunks that made her take a second look at his impressive physique. She paddled languidly through the water as Nicholai moved with sure, strong strokes. Several times he disappeared beneath the surface, popping back up with a shell or a bit of sea glass to show her.

At one point, they both drifted lazily on their backs, staring up at the impossibly blue sky.

"I can't remember the last time I just relaxed," she murmured.

"I know when I did. Paris."

The answer surprised her enough that she lost her buoyancy and righted herself in the water.

"Really?"

"Yes." He treaded water next to her, his eyes boring into hers. "That was the first night in a long time where I could just be myself. Part of it was you not knowing who I was. But a large part of that was you, Madeline."

"Nicholai…"

He reached out, his fingertips trailing over her cheek. "For the next four days, I want to be those two people we were on the roof that night."

"Just Nick?"

"Just Nick," he repeated with a small smile, "and Madeline. No titles, no crown, no paparazzi—"

"Or pompous investors?"

"Or pompous investors," Nicholai agreed with a chuckle. "I care about you a great deal, Madeline. Would you join me in that? Just being us for a few days?"

She swam closer until their legs brushed against each other. She reached up, cupped his face.

"I'd like that very much."

He leaned down and sealed his lips over hers. She surrendered herself to the moment, the novel sensation of kissing a man she cared deeply about while balancing in the waves of a far-flung tropical getaway.

Yet even as he deepened the kiss, hugged her

closer against him, she couldn't ignore the whisper of warning across the back of her neck at the finality she had heard in his words. The resignation that, after their time in Bora Bora, their time together would be over.

It was one of those incredible days that seemed to extend forever and yet slipped by in the blink of an eye. They kayaked out to the breakers, dozed on the hammock stretched out over the water and indulged in a long soak in the hot tub on the patio. Dusk seeped into the sky with a rainbow of colors, from rosy pink and deep violet to fiery orange and the deep blue hint of night spreading up from the east.

Madeline had just finished showering and stepped out onto the patio as a butler finished laying the table. On the white tablecloth, a low candle flickered next to a vase holding a single red rose. The butler poured them each a glass of wine, bowed and departed as silently as he had arrived. They savored *poisson cru*, succulent fish marinated in lime and coconut milk and served on a bed of onions, cucumber and tomatoes, grilled mahi-mahi and *po'e*, a baked pudding, for dessert.

"I don't think I can move."

Nicholai laughed. "Perhaps I should ask the palace chef to replicate some of the recipes."

Madeline made a soft humming noise in response. Allowed herself the indulgence of imagining a future where she would dine at the palace with Nicholai as his true bride.

Stars winked into existence overhead, peppering the night sky with their glittering brilliance. Madeline breathed in, exhaled as she savored pure contentment.

"You know, when we were in Paris, the one thing that disappointed me about that night was that I could only see a few stars."

"I'm glad to know that was the only thing that disappointed you."

Madeline shot him a saucy smile. "How could I not be impressed by your Superman routine?"

He rubbed the back of his neck in a self-conscious gesture. "I was worried about you."

"And you didn't even know who I was." Whether it was the wine or the ambience or the man sitting next to her, the magnitude of what she had just said hit her. "You really are a good man."

Nicholai started, a frown crossing his face. "What?"

"You literally jumped from a balcony to help someone you thought was in need. When our picture showed up in the papers, you were worried about the effect it would have on Kelna instead of yourself." She smiled at him. "I don't think there are many men like you left in the world."

He stared out over the darkening scene. Tendons tightened in his neck.

"Nicholai?"

"You say I'm honorable. Except what I'm thinking right now is far from honorable."

"Tell me," she urged softly.

He pulled his phone from his pocket, his fingers tapping across the screen. A moment later, the lilting strains of an orchestra filled the air. He stood, placing his phone on the table and extending a hand to her.

"Dance with me."

She took his outstretched hand, let him tug her to her feet and pull her close as they swayed on the patio against the darkening sky blending into the ocean. She rested her cheek on his chest, felt the beat of his heart against her skin. She pressed a little closer, wanting to savor his woodsy scent, the strength of his embrace, all the details she feared would one day fade from memory.

"Madeline…"

She looked up into eyes that echoed both her own wants and fears.

"Stay with me tonight."

She rose up on her toes and let her kiss serve as her answer.

Nicholai watched the sun rise over the waters of the lagoon. He'd fallen asleep last night with Madeline in his arms, the most content he could ever remember being. He'd awoken at dawn with her body curved against his, her breathing soft against his chest.

Since that first night, they'd spent every night together. Their days had been filled with exploring the resort, hiking the nature reserve, swimming in the waters of the lagoon, their adventures interrupted only by exquisite meals and long stretches of doing absolutely nothing other than lounging on the patio or relaxing in the hot tub.

One of his most vivid memories had been lying in the hammock with Madeline's head on his shoulder as she had read one of her classic novels and he'd thumbed through a mystery he had been meaning to read for well over a year. The water lapping beneath them, and the sky stretching above them, had brought him a peace he hadn't even known he'd been searching for.

A peace that had evaporated with the coming dawn.

Inside, a war raged on. A selfish part of his character, one he hadn't even fully known existed, demanded that he ask Madeline to stay. To become his fiancée for real and the future queen of Kelna.

But the rational part, the man his father had raised him to be, argued against temptation. Madeline deserved a normal life. She deserved to have the career she had worked so hard for.

He scrubbed a hand over his face as her words from their drive came back to him.

I'm going to miss this place...

Would she miss it enough to consider giving them a chance? To stay and see if their relationship could turn into something more? Something permanent?

The buzzing of his phone interrupted his thoughts. Frowning when he saw the prime minister's name on the screen, he answered.

"Yes?"

"Your Highness." Dario's tone was grim. "The duchess is engaged."

"Excuse me?"

"The Duchess. You met and were photographed with her at the ball."

"Oh." He vaguely remembered the blonde woman Dario had introduced him to shortly after the start of the ball. She'd been pleasant to talk to. But there had been no spark, nothing beyond two professionals meeting and considering a mutually beneficial arrangement.

"Forgive my impudence, Your Highness, but how much longer are you going to continue this charade?"

Nicholai's fingers tightened on the phone. "I told you. As long as it takes."

"For the country or yourself?"

"Watch yourself, Prime Minister." Nicholai's voice turned to ice. "I don't take kindly to being questioned in such a manner."

"And I don't enjoy doing it. But it's been almost a month."

"I said a month, possibly two."

"The longer you wait, the harder it will be to move on."

"You mean select a wife from your list of potential candidates?"

"A list you agreed to, Your Highness," Dario replied, his voice a step away from defiance. "Are you considering turning this pretense into a real engagement? With a woman you told me yourself has no interest in residing in Kelna?"

"What I am considering or not is not your concern."

"Given that you must receive Parliament's approval on your choice of a wife while meeting the requirements of the Marriage Law, it is very much my concern."

"Approval you have already voiced publicly." Dario's silence gave Nicholai a small sense of satisfaction. "I understand the law, Prime Minister. I will wed within the year of assuming the throne. But who I choose—"

A creak sounded behind him. Dread filled his chest with a heavy weight.

"I'll call you back."

Steeling himself, he stood and turned. Madeline stood framed in the doorway. Dressed in white cotton shorts and a blue tank top, with her hair in a tousled blond halo around her face, she looked beautiful.

And heartbroken, he realized as the weight grew and dragged his heart down with it.

"What did you hear?"

"Enough."

"Madeline—"

He reached for her. She flinched and stepped back.

"There's a *law* that requires you to marry?"

His hands fell to his sides. "Yes."

"Why didn't you tell me?"

"It's an old law. One that hasn't been enforced for nearly two-hundred years. The Kings before me were much older and already married before they ascended the throne."

"So what?"

"When the prime minister told me about it after my father's diagnosis, we agreed it was best not to draw public attention to it. We wanted the future queen to be..."

"Someone from your list of potential candidates?"

The bitterness in her tone alarmed him. She wrapped her arms about her waist as if to shield herself from him.

"You only heard part of the conversation."

"I heard enough. When you kissed me in Paris and told me you weren't free to pursue anything, it's because you were looking for a wife like you were shopping for groceries."

Irritated by her casual dismissal of the conundrum he faced, he shoved his hands in his pockets. "It wasn't my first choice. But, Madeline, I'd just learned that my father was dying and I had to not only take over the throne but marry, too. When the prime minister offered to compile a list of candidates, it seemed like the right choice."

"What changed?" Her lips parted as the color disappeared from her face. "The ball. The blonde woman he introduced you to, the duchess. She was on the list, wasn't she?"

His jaw hardened. "Yes."

"But I wasn't."

"No." The word was torn from someplace deep inside him. He wanted to lie, to soothe away the pain on her face. "But I've come to care about you, Madeline. Deeply. I want to try and make this into something permanent."

"Do you? Or do you just want me because I'm convenient? Because I can get you something you want?"

Hurt made his chest ache. "Do you truly believe I would do that?"

"I don't know what to believe. I've believed before, and I've gotten hurt."

His gut clenched at being compared to Alex. Realizing her mistake, Madeline hastened to rephrase her words.

"I only meant—"

"You don't need to explain."

He shook his head. Of all the ways he'd pictured the morning going, this had not been one of them. He had envisioned telling Madeline how much he cared, that he wanted a chance for them to see where this relationship could take them.

Nowhere.

He had hurt her too much, and she him.

"I'll arrange for you to fly home."

"Home," she echoed.

"Yes. Kansas City." He inclined his head to her even as his heart fell to his knees. "Thank you, Miss Delvine, for all of your help."

And then he turned and walked away from the woman he loved.

CHAPTER SIXTEEN

MADELINE TAPPED HER pen against her desk. The steady rhythm echoed in the empty office. It had been over a week since she had returned from Bora Bora. The media had gone blissfully silent, distracted by a scandal involving an international pop star. Aside from a news blip about one other bridge in Kelna being found unsafe and in need of repair, the world had temporarily moved on from their obsession with the tiny Adriatic country.

Everyone, that is, except her.

Whenever she thought back to those last moments on the patio with the rising sun illuminating Nicholai's handsome, solemn expression, grief hit her just as it had when he'd walked away.

She had thought Nicholai was going to join her on the flight home. But when the car had pulled up, he had come out only to say goodbye, telling her that he was catching a different flight that would take him west and back to Kelna faster than going east would. She had accepted his excuse, contemplated kissing him one last time, and then decided it would be too painful for both of them. She'd gotten in the car and let herself be driven away without a backward glance.

A move she had almost instantly regretted, but hadn't been able to bring herself to fix.

The tapping of her pen intensified. She'd let her own hurt and past fears get the better of her. Had judged him harshly in the moment instead of placing herself in his shoes. She knew Nicholai. Knew the kind of man he was. The pain on his face when she'd insinuated he was anything like Alex haunted her every night.

That and running away instead of fighting.

Why had she not told him the true depth of her feelings? Because she was scared? Scared that he wouldn't feel the same way? Frightened that loving him and even contemplating the possibility of somehow making a relationship work would mean repeating past mistakes and forfeiting independence?

Her fear, rooted in her past, had overridden what she'd known both in her heart and her mind. Nicholai was not Alex. Not her father. Would things have been different if she had shared that, somewhere along the way, she'd fallen in love with him? That his commitment to his people, the honor he brought to his role, the way he had treated her like a partner even in the midst of their charade, had pulled her deeper into the emotions he had awakened that first night in Paris?

She sighed and leaned back into her chair, letting her head fall against the headrest. She regretted it now, and yet still couldn't bring herself to call him. To take that final step.

"There you are."

Madeline let out a little shriek and whirled around. Her mother stood behind her, hands on her hips, with that motherly look that conveyed Madeline was in trouble etched onto her porcelain skin.

"Hey, Mom."

"Don't 'Hey, Mom' me." Stacey Delvine marched up to her daughter's desk and sat down in the chair across from her. "It's time you told me what's going on."

Madeline nodded. "Yeah."

Stacey blinked. "I was expecting more of a fight."

Madeline let out a watery laugh. "I don't think I have any fight left in me."

Stacey's eyes narrowed.

"Has he hurt you?"

"What?"

"That boy. Has he hurt you?"

"The boy you're referring to is a prince."

"I don't care if he's the King of England. Did he hurt you?"

Madeline sucked in a shuddering breath. "Yes. But not in the way you think."

She told her mother everything, starting from the night in Paris with Nicholai's superhuman jump onto the rooftop, how the illicit kiss on the terrace had happened, the fake engagement, all the way up to that horrid morning in Bora Bora when they had parted ways.

Stacey sat back in her chair. "Well."

"Yeah."

"Quite a mess."

"Mild way of putting it."

"What are you going to do?"

Madeline massaged her temples as a headache began to form. "I don't know, Mom. This feels different than what I went through with Alex."

"It is different." Stacey leaned forward. "Alex wanted to control you. From what you've told me, Nicholai is the opposite. He knows you. He cares for you."

"I thought he did. But the law...the *list*..."

"I'm not saying he handled things well." Stacey cocked her head. "But do you think he really concealed all of that to hurt you? That he was searching for a wife all this time?"

"No."

"Then, time for the most difficult question of all." Stacey gathered Madeline's hands in hers. "Do you truly believe he agreed to the engagement simply because you were a convenience? Or because, even in the beginning, he wanted you in his life?"

She stared down at her mother's hands wrapped around her own. The touch grounded her, allowed her to breathe and push away the mess of insecurities and heartache. She looked out the window at the familiar sights of the city that had been her home for so long. The tower of the World War I museum, smoke spilling over the stone rim from the eternal flame. The circular fountain outside the impressive stone facade of Union Station. The tracks of the streetcar that whisked Kansas Citians and tourists alike up to the River Market. Her eyes strayed to a brick office building, one of the first projects she had worked on as an intern.

If she looked past her own hurt and really thought about giving a relationship with Nicholai a shot, she knew it would mean letting go of some things she cared deeply about. It made her sad, but in a bittersweet way. Saying good-bye to one stage as she stood on the precipice of a change she knew could bring her and Nicholai great happiness.

"You love him."

Madeline looked at her mother with heartbroken eyes. "I do. I was so insistent on being alone for a while, on not dating, on not forming any romantic attachments. I thought that's what I needed. But looking back on it, it was more to protect myself. I fell for Alex and ignored the warning signs because he was familiar. Easy. I wanted to be married. I wanted my own family. Wanted the same kind of stability Paul brought to our family, the dream of being a wife and mother. And I lost myself in that." She ran her hands through her hair.

"Yet I'm now in love with a man whose future wife must do exactly that. Surrender herself to a rule, to an entire country."

When Stacey spoke, her voice was thick with tears. "I can't think of a single good thing in my life that has not required some sort of sacrifice. Even being a mother meant I had to give some things up."

"I know. I don't want to end up in the same position you were forced into by...him."

Even now, all these years later, she couldn't bring herself to call the man who had treated them so horribly by the title of *father*. "You told me you gave up everything, and all he did was take more and more."

"You truly think Nicholai would do that to you?"

"No. But being a queen... The day that I went to the hospital was one of the most humbling experiences of my life. And I know moments like that are not the norm. But they could happen at any time. Where I might have to leave my work, my own children, to serve the people." Her heart ached. "I'm coming to understand, just a little bit, the pressure that Nicholai feels to lead. To be the best representative he can be. Even if he would agree to try again, I don't know if I'm strong enough to do that."

Stacey reached over and squeezed her daughter's hand. "During a faked engagement, you stood up to the international press and spent hours with a frightened girl in a hospital. You didn't buckle under the pressure of an ex giving a tell-all interview."

"Yeah. But that was a few weeks. I don't know if I can keep that up for years on end."

"Darling, tomorrow J.T. might lose the business. The economy might collapse. War could break out. Yes," Stacey said as she reached up and smoothed a curl back from Madeline's face, "know your strengths. Know your weaknesses. Know what your limits are. But what I see is a young woman more than capable of seizing that life with both hands and making the most of it next to the man she loves. And she's letting herself be held back by fear."

The truth of her mother's words hit her hard.

"Well. When you say it like that, suddenly it all makes sense."

"Which is why you should have come to me sooner."

Madeline laughed. "I should have. But I didn't want to betray his confidence."

"I understand that." Stacey blinked back tears. "Believe me, I am not a fan of my daughter moving halfway around the world. And maybe you'll go and talk to Nicholai, and you won't be on the same page."

The possibility nearly tore Madeline in two. "I hurt him, Mom."

"And he hurt you. If you stay together, it will

happen again. But," Stacey added softly, "if you love each other, if you work through those hurts together, it can lead to an even greater love."

"I love him," Madeline whispered softly. Then, as a smile stole over her face, she said it louder.

"I'm in love with a prince."

Nicholai stared at the rapidly forming skeleton of the new bridge. He saw the stone foundation, the massive pillars, the long threads of iron that would be laid into the cement. He saw it all, but hardly any of it registered.

"Your Highness?"

Nicholai turned to the newly appointed bridge inspector at his side.

"I apologize. My mind was elsewhere. You were telling me of the tentative construction schedule."

The inspector nodded enthusiastically.

"Yes, we expect for it to be ready in six months."

"And done to code?"

"Yes." The inspector's expression turned grave. "I will not make the same mistakes as my predecessor."

Nicholai offered his hand to the young woman. "I know the transportation director chose well."

He moved on to tour the rest of the site, conscious of the photographers huddling. There had been an audible murmur of disappointment when he'd emerged from the royal car alone.

Even though their vacation had been uninterrupted, it hadn't stopped photos of their private plane leaving Kansas City and then Los Angeles from making the rounds on social media.

Public Affairs had begun to forward him the various articles and trending posts in a daily report. Yesterday's report had included a picture of Madeline with her mother walking down an avenue of trees at the Nelson. Their arms had been entwined, smiles wreathing their faces. Stacey Delvine was still a beautiful woman, and the relationship between the two was clear in the pointed chin, the slight tilt to their nose, their dark brows a pleasant contrast to their blond hair.

Another regret. Not meeting the family that had raised such an incredible woman. A woman he'd let get away because, as he'd made his own plans, he hadn't opened up, hadn't confided in Madeline and told her everything until it was too late.

The tour of the site completed, Nicholai returned to the palace. The next few hours flew by as he dealt with one matter after another.

A knock on his door made him blink.

"Enter."

Eviana walked in with a tray in her hands. "It's almost seven."

He glanced at the bay of windows. "It's still light outside."

"When was the last time you ate?"

He glanced at his watch, frowned. "I think breakfast."

Eviana sighed and set the tray down in front of him. The delicious aroma of roasted chicken and rice wafted up from the covered dish.

"Thank you."

Eviana prowled about the room, stopping to examine a book or one of the folders he had left out.

"Was there something else?"

"What happened between you and Madeline on your vacation?"

Nicholai looked at her with narrowed eyes.

"What do you mean?"

"Don't give me that. Ever since you came back, you've been moping around like a lovesick teenager."

"I'm a prince. I don't mope."

Eviana's face softened. "Nicholai, you look like you've lost your best friend. What's wrong?"

No longer hungry, and resigned that his sister wouldn't rest until she'd discovered the true story one way or another, Nicholai set the fork down.

"In a week or so, Madeline and I will announce the end of our engagement."

Eviana's eyes bugged out of her head. "What?"

"Don't play coy, Eviana. You had to have suspected that Madeline and I had an arrangement, not a true engagement."

"I had a pretty good idea of why you were suddenly engaged to someone I had barely met, but you two are good together. Good for Kelna." She slammed her hands down on the desk and leaned forward. "You're in love with her."

Nicholai's heart twisted in his chest. "Yes."

"And she loves you."

"She cares for me."

"She loves you," Eviana repeated.

"Whether or not she does is irrelevant."

"Did you tell her how you feel? Did you ask her to consider being your actual fiancée?"

He thought back to their last conversation on the patio of the bungalow. Relived those final, gut-wrenching moments.

"I alluded to it, yes."

"But you didn't ask."

"She learned about the Marriage Law and the list of candidates the prime minister composed. She said she didn't know if she could trust that I wasn't asking for our relationship to become real because I cared about her or because it was convenient." He pushed the memory out of his head. "Besides, she loves her career. I doubt she would give that up."

"Why can't she do something related to architecture here?"

Nicholai gestured to the bustling construction site on the horizon. "Kelna is growing, Eviana. faster than any of us anticipated. I can barely keep up with things as it is. And when Father…" He breathed in deep. "When Father passes, my responsibilities will increase even more."

"Why haven't you asked me?"

Nicholai looked at the sister. "What?"

"Why haven't you asked me for more help?" She almost sounded hurt.

Nicholai frowned. "You have your own life. The charities you work with, the public appearances—"

"Which does take up a lot of my time, yes. But it's not nearly the amount of work compared to the load you carry."

Nicholai rubbed the back of his neck. "I never thought to ask."

Eviana looked down at the desk, traced her finger across the pattern on the wood.

"I sometimes wondered if it's because you didn't trust me."

"Nothing could be further from the truth." His eyes moved back to the construction site. "It was just always the expectation that I would take over one day. When Father got sick about the same time that Kelna began expanding, I became so focused on what I had to do that I couldn't see anything else."

"You always were independent."

His lips worked at the corners. "So is Madeline. Eviana, I can't ask her to give up her life."

"What if it's not giving up her life but adapting, changing it? Think about it, Nicholai. If I were to take on some of the duties that you currently handle, and then Madeline takes over some as the future queen, that will be three instead of one."

"Even if we were to share duties, that doesn't solve the problem of her career."

"There are at least two architecture firms right here in Lepa Plavi. Have Madeline take on the occasional project that she wants, or maybe even serve as a consultant for her firm, make time for her to be able to do what she loves."

He almost didn't want to entertain the possibility, allow himself to hope. "I don't know if she can forgive me for not confiding in her sooner. If she can believe that I care about her for her and not because of some archaic law."

"And she may say no. But don't you owe it to her to give her that chance, to hear all the possible options and decide for herself?"

"And what about you, Eviana? This would be taking on a massive responsibility. It'll change your life as well."

She nodded. "It would. And no, it's not what I envisioned for my life." She shrugged. "I would be lying if I said it was my first choice, but I would rather have some of what I wanted and help lead than see you shoulder the burden alone. Especially if it means letting someone like Madeline get away."

"She really is something."

"When I heard her defend Amara at the press conference, I knew I liked her as a woman. And then, when she held that little girl at the hospital, I liked her as a leader for our people." She moved to Nicholai and flung her arms around his neck just like she had when she'd been a little girl. "You carry so much weight for our family. It's time to share the burden and finally go after something you want."

He returned her hug, fought past the tightness in his throat as he spoke.

"Thank you."

Suddenly filled with an iron resolve, he moved to his desk.

"I have two meetings tomorrow—"

"I'll cover them."

"I'll miss the economic forum."

Eviana wrinkled her nose. "Not my favorite, but I'll manage."

"Thank you." He pulled open his drawer. "Could I get your opinion?"

"Sure, on what?"

Her eyes widened as he pulled out a blue jewelry box. "I thought she already had a ring."

"One picked out by Public Affairs."

"How long have you been holding on to this?"

"A little over a week."

He flipped open the lid, satisfaction curling through him at Eviana's delighted gasp.

"Nicholai…it's perfect."

"Let's hope Madeline thinks so, too." He shot her a sudden, confident smile. "Hopefully the next time I see you, I'll have a princess by my side."

CHAPTER SEVENTEEN

"MESSAGE CAME THROUGH for you."

Frowning, she took the slip of paper J.T. held out to her. "From who?"

"Potential client. They really liked your design of the ballroom and are wanting to talk to you about a similar project."

Madeline looked at the paper. "They want to meet at the Nelson?"

J.T. gave her an encouraging smile. "I told them it was an inspirational site for you and your work. I can vouch for them. Nothing sinister."

Madeline laughed even as she rolled her eyes. "The fact that you have to clarify it's nothing sinister makes me wonder what you're up to."

J.T. sobered. "I know the last month has been rough on you, kid."

Madeline struggled to keep her smile in place even as her heart twisted inside her chest.

"Nothing I can't handle."

She nearly squirmed under J.T.'s somber gaze. The man usually had the jovialness of Santa Claus, but when he chose to, he could be frighteningly perceptive.

"I know there's more to this engagement than you're telling me."

She lifted her shoulders and tried to give him an enigmatic smile.

"I'm worried you're going to get hurt again."

His kind words chipped away at her stubbornness. "I think it's too late for that. But I made choices. And this time... Nicholai isn't like Alex."

Just saying his name hurt. But no matter what happened, she would not regret her time with him.

Her answer seemed to satisfy an unspoken question. "Okay." He nodded toward the slip of paper. "Got time to meet with them in an hour?"

She glanced at her computer. With the ballroom construction project on hold, and the other projects the team had been working on nearly completed, she had experienced an unusual and yet very necessary decline in demands on her time.

"Sure."

"Great." J.T.'s eyes twinkled. "Let me know what you think."

She hesitated. "Would you ever let someone be a consultant?"

J.T. brows shot up.

"Consultant?"

"Yeah." The idea took hold, a bridge between a life she had never envisioned and the work she loved. The look he gave her made her think that he knew exactly what she was alluding to.

"For you? Absolutely." He smiled down at her with fatherly pride. "You are one of the most creative, talented architects I've ever had the pleasure of working with."

She swallowed past the lump in her throat. "Thank you."

"But something I've learned in my sixty-two years on this earth is that sometimes the life we thought we were going to have isn't what's meant to be. That doesn't mean we can't still make it into something we love."

"You're wise in your old age."

He squeezed her shoulder even as he narrowed his eyes at her. "Off with you, young lady. Go meet that client."

She waited until J.T. walked away before she went online and typed in Nicholai's name. A new story posted early yesterday afternoon included pictures of Nicholai touring the bridge construction site, speaking with the new inspector, and shaking hands with some of the construction crew. He looked tired, his lips drawn tight, lines edged deep into the skin around his eyes.

Was he ill? Or had he been having trouble sleeping, just as she had, since they'd parted? After her conversation with her mother, she had decided to reach out to Nicholai and apologize. Then, whether he forgave her or not, she would tell him she loved him. If he rejected her, then she could at least walk away knowing she'd done everything she could.

Now, she thought grimly, she just needed to find the courage to make the call.

She arrived at the Nelson and parked along the side street. She could glimpse the south entrance between the trees. Glancing at her watch, she realized she still had ten minutes or so before she met the client at the base of the stairs.

It was after five, and the museum had closed for the day. Dark clouds heavy with rain hung in the sky, chasing people from the lawn. She reached into the back of her car for an umbrella. Perhaps after meeting the client, she could convince him or her to join her for a drink at a restaurant on the Plaza to discuss whatever project they had pitched to J.T.

She followed the winding path of one of the sidewalks that ran between a low stone wall and majestic trees that stretched up to the stormy sky. The distant sounds of traffic and city life faded as she mentally composed what she would say when she called Nicholai.

Nicholai, I think I'm in love with you.

No, too abrupt.

Remember how I said I couldn't picture giving up my career? What if I found a way to make it work while being in Kelna?

So lost in her thoughts was she that she didn't

see the man standing in front of her until she ran smack into him.

"Oh! I apologize, I…"

Her voice faded as she stared up into Nicholai's handsome face.

"Hello, Madeline."

"Nicholai?"

She launched herself at him, flinging her arms around his neck, burying her face against his shoulder. His scent enveloped her, woodsy with that hint of spice, a fragrance that had become so familiar in such a short time. He crushed her against him, brushed his cheek against hers, caressed her hair.

"I missed you."

"I missed you, too."

He drew back, cradled her chin in one hand and kissed her. Her eyes fluttered shut, tears clinging to her lashes as the last bands of tension wrapped around her heart loosened and fell away.

Thunder grumbled overhead. Rain started to fall, the leafy branches overhead providing some shelter.

They broke apart. Madeline tilted her head back and laughed.

"I've always wanted to be kissed in the rain."

He ran his thumb over her lower lip. "I'm glad I could do that for you."

"Seriously, though, Nicholai, what are you doing here? Where's your security team?"

He gestured to the trees bordering the road that

ran alongside the museum. "Close by. It took some convincing for them to not accompany me up here."

She glanced at her watch and sucked in a breath. "Oh. I have to meet a client—"

"Interested in a new venture with Forge?"

Her lips curved up. "J.T. knew this whole time, didn't he?"

"I called him yesterday and asked him for a favor."

Her fingers reached up, traced the sharp line of his jaw, the coarse stubble on his chin, then down his neck before laying her hand over his heart. The steady beat beneath her palm summoned the memories of their time in Bora Bora, the intimacy of lying side by side and the simplicity of enjoying each other's company.

"You could have just called or texted me."

"This seemed more romantic." He nodded to the stone steps and giant birdies standing proudly on the lawn. "I couldn't pass up the chance to see the larger-than-life shuttlecocks in person."

She laughed as he grabbed her hand and tugged her down the lane. The cool mist turned into big raindrops. Belatedly, she remembered the umbrella and popped it open, holding it above both their heads as the rain drummed steadily on the fabric.

"When we last spoke, I told you I cared about you."

Her pulse accelerated.

"You did. And I—"

"Wait."

He stopped, tugged her around to face him.

"The first time I saw you, I thought I was going to have to save your life." He silenced her laugh with a sweet kiss. "But I was wrong. You're the one who ended up saving me, Madeline."

Confused, she leaned back. "How?"

"I wasn't dealing well with the change in my life. My father's illness, Kelna's expansion, the new port. I was so focused on my responsibilities, on the ways things used to be, that I couldn't see the possibilities in the future." He smoothed a lock of hair back from her face. "I also didn't realize how much my own need to control something in my life was preventing me from asking for help."

"I'm not exactly one to judge on that front."

"No," he agreed with a slight smile. "But you've made me a better leader, Madeline. You showed me the value in slowing down, in enjoying my life instead of just moving through it without stopping to look at what was around me."

One tear escaped and traced a hot trail down her cheek.

"Nicholai…" She swallowed hard. "Thank you. Although you helped me grow, too, you know."

"Oh?"

"I was so focused on my need for familiarity that I closed myself off to so many possibilities. And then you introduced me to your beautiful country and I..." Her voice trailed off as she blinked back tears. "It pushed me out of my comfort zone. I started looking around and seeing things beyond my own interpretations. All of the meetings and commitments I saw at first as confining, but then I saw what a difference they made. What a difference you make. I love my work and what I do." A tear slid down her cheek. "But I loved being a part of something bigger, too."

He brushed his finger over her cheek. "Don't cry, *moja ljubav*."

"They're not sad tears, I promise." She swallowed. "I have a question to ask."

"Which you can. After me."

With that pronouncement, he dropped to one knee. The rapid beat of her heart catapulted into a gallop, one that thundered so loudly in her ears she barely heard the words that came out of his mouth. He released her hand and pulled a jewelry box out of his pocket. He flipped the lid. Her hand flew up to her mouth.

Could she have imagined a more perfect ring? Delicate silver, fashioned into three strands that wove over each other in an elegant braid, made up the band, with a square blue topaz sitting on top and surrounded by the tiniest drops of diamonds.

"This belonged to my mother. She was much loved as a queen." Nicholai glanced down at the ring, then back to her, his heart in his eyes. "I knew I would one day marry. I wondered if I would have the luxury of a marriage based on affection. When I told you in Bora Bora that I cared about you, I lied. I love you, Madeline. I never pictured that I would fall so deeply in love with the woman I want to be my wife, my queen and the mother of our children. Will you marry me?"

Barely had the words left his mouth before she leaned down and kissed him. The umbrella tumbled to the ground, forgotten as the rain drenched them.

"Yes," she breathed against his lips. "Yes, Nicholai. I love you. I love you so much."

"I almost lost you." He gripped her tight, kissed her cheeks, her neck, before holding her tight in his arms. "At first, I told myself I was doing the right thing letting you go. Not making you choose between a life here and a life with me."

"But this is different." She ran a hand through his hair, smoothing the wet locks back from his forehead. "That was the lesson I had to learn. When you love someone and you want to be with them, there's sacrifice. Compromise. And I want to be with you, Nicholai."

He slipped the ring on her finger.

"Your mother will be relieved."

"My mother?" Madeline echoed.

"I called her. I asked her blessing for your hand. She said she's going to miss you and she'd toss me in the river if I hurt you."

Madeline choked out a laugh. "Sounds like her."

"Promising her her own mother-in-law's quarters, available for her exclusive use whenever she wanted to visit, seemed to help."

"Another expansion to the palace?"

"More a renovation of existing rooms. Which reminds me…" He brought her hand up to his mouth, kissed the tips of her fingers. "I'd like to add an office."

"An office?"

"For you. If you're interested, there are two architecture firms in Lepa Plavi, as well as an opening with the country's development authority."

The hope that had taken root in her chest during her earlier conversation with J.T. now bloomed, filling her with an elation so bright it made her lightheaded.

"But what about serving as queen?"

"My sister and I talked. Kelna is growing, and so are the needs of its people. She has agreed to step up and assume more of the royal duties. Instead of being just one or two, we'll be three, perhaps four if she decides to marry."

"And you're okay with that?"

"I know I'm asking you to give up a lot, Madeline. I can't solve the problems of the media, public scrutiny, having to have a security guard when you travel. But I can offer you a way to do what you love and continue to make a difference." His thumb brushed away a drop on her cheek. "Are these more tears or raindrops?"

"Probably both," she said as she smiled. "I asked J.T. before I came here if I could be a consultant. I was going to call you this weekend and tell you I love you, that I wanted to see if we could make this work."

He stared down at her. "You were going to give up your career? For me?"

"Not give up. Just…change things. I want to be with you, Nicholai. I need to draw, to design. But I also want to do more giving back. I fell in love with you, but I also fell in love with your country. I want to serve it as best I can."

"I have no doubt you will." Nicholai looked up as the rain started to fall harder. "And now, Princess Madeline, it's time to get inside."

She let out a shriek of laughter as he scooped her up into his arms and carried her down the lane. She leaned up and kissed his cheek.

"Do you remember in Paris when I said it didn't get more fairy-tale than that moment?"

"I do."

"I was wrong," she said on a sigh of happiness.

"As was I." He pressed a kiss to her forehead. "Here's to happily-ever-after, Your Highness."

EPILOGUE

Eighteen months later

THE SUN ROSE above the palace, casting a rosy glow over the walls as it slid high above the mountains to the east.

Madeline sighed and reclined in her chair. She'd woken up before dawn, too excited to sleep. In just a few hours, she would say "I do" and officially be crowned as Queen Madeline Adamović.

Nicholai's wife.

After he'd officially proposed, he'd spent the night at her apartment. The next morning, Stacey had joined them to meet her future son-in-law. There had been lots of tears, hugs and questions about Kelna. Seeing her mother at ease with Nicholai in a way she'd never been with Alex had made Madeline even happier, a feat she hadn't thought possible.

They'd flown back to Kelna shortly after to confess their charade to Ivan. The King had simply smiled and embraced them both.

"I knew you would find your way eventually."

Nicholai had invited her to meet with the prime minister with him, a sign to show that he would work on no longer doing everything alone. They'd sat before the stern-faced man, hands laced together, as they'd told him of their commitment to each other.

"The women on your list were meant to lead Kelna." Nicholai had looked at Madeline, love shining from his eyes, and squeezed her hand. "Madeline put her life on hold and her reputation on the line to help our country in a time of need. She served our children during a dark hour. She loves Kelna as if she were born here." He'd looked back to Dario. "What more could I or the people want in a queen?"

Nicholai still maintained that Madeline had imagined the flicker of emotion in Dario's eyes. Regardless, he had agreed to support their engagement and their marriage.

The next few months had sped by. Madeline had continued to work on the ballroom with the team from Forge, mostly through remote work, but with occasional trips back to Kansas City. Ivan had lived long enough to see construction begin before he had finally succumbed to his illness.

Madeline's hands tightened on her mug. Losing his father had hit Nicholai hard. But they'd leaned on each other and Eviana, forming their own tight-knit family as the nation had mourned with them.

The decision to postpone the wedding had been

an easy one. They'd set it for one day after the anniversary of when Nicholai had been crowned king, a nod to the Marriage Law that had been quietly repealed by Parliament a month after Nicholai and Madeline had reunited.

I'm getting married today.

She smiled and let her head fall back as she soaked up the warmth of the rising sun.

A shadow fell across her.

"Good morning."

"Nicholai!" Laughing, she set her mug down and stood. "It's bad luck to see the bride before the wedding."

"I thought that was seeing you in your dress." He leaned down and kissed her. "I couldn't start my day without you."

Sighing happily, she leaned into his embrace. "Just a few hours."

"And then a week of nothing but sun, sand and waves."

"I'm excited to go back."

She felt his smile against her hair. "It will definitely have a happier ending than the last time we were in Bora Bora."

Nicholai suddenly tensed.

"What is it?"

He held a finger to his lips and leaned over the railing. Madeline turned to see Eviana by the evergreen trees. And she wasn't alone. A man stood with his back to them, hands gesturing wildly as Eviana glared at him. She leaned in and said something too low for them to hear. Judging by her angry expression, though, it wasn't anything pleasant.

"I should go down there," Nicholai growled as Eviana stalked off, leaving the man staring after her.

"She's a big girl. And she respects you. She'll come to you if she needs help."

Although she would be sure to check in with her maid of honor before the ceremony started. Ever since Eviana had returned from a sabbatical three months ago, she'd been quieter, more subdued. Perhaps the young man who was now marching off in the opposite direction had something to do with her morose mood. "Maybe." Nicholai sighed and turned back to her. "Given how I feel about my baby sister talking to a man, I can only imagine how I'm going to feel if we have a daughter."

"Maybe we can find out next year," she teased as she looped her arms around his neck.

"Maybe." He smiled down at her. "Wedding first. I'm very much looking forward to sliding that wedding band on your finger and letting the world know you're mine."

"So we can live happily ever after?" Madeline laughed as Nicholai responded to her teasing by sweeping her into his arms.

He leaned down, his lips brushing hers.

"Ever after and always."

* * * * *